United
Seventh Grade

Alyssa Raffaele

This book is dedicated to every
seventh grader in the world.

1

My name is Nines, and I was chosen by my classmates to tell you the story of how a small town canceled seventh grade, and how we became The United Seventh Grade of America. My classmates selected me because I have always been good at writing; in fact, I kept a record of the events as they unfolded – the events, which united us one and all.

I am writing in first person narrative because it seems most natural, but Samantha and Julian are here with me, and Elliot, Brian and Mark are on their way, so if it seems like I am suddenly **omniscient**, and you are wondering how I could possibly know what everyone is thinking or feeling or seeing, it's because they are sitting right here next to me as I write, and they want to make sure their story is told.

Everyone's story matters.

I've added a glossary at the back of the book, listing definitions for words you might not have seen before. Glossary words are in **bold**.

Right now Samantha is sitting on top of me and nagging me about something she needs to write. I have to do it because she is huge and it hurts. She's not really huge, just tall, but she looks huge to me because I am scrawny and short. She made me write that but now I have to let her write something.

Hi, it's Sam. I just want to give you guys a description of Nines. She will not talk about herself because she is too shy, so I think you should know a little bit about her before you read our story. Nines is small and very pretty. Her skin is the color of beach sand in Cape Cod. Her nose is thin and straight, which I always notice because my nose is totally big. Her hair is brown and always messy because she never brushes it during the day. She normally wears it in two barrettes, one on each side of her head. She wears no makeup, but I do.

Julian and Nines are the same height (short), and Elliot and I are the same height (tall). Julian's skin is dark, Nines is medium (in makeup language, "medium beige" would be the best color for her foundation), Elliot has dirty-blonde shaggy hair, and I am naturally blonde and light-skinned.

Thank you, Sam. Now, back to our story.

The name Nines was given to me by my classmates and teachers at Shadyside School. My real name is Ninevah. Both of my parents are archaeologists, and they named me after the famous, ancient Mesopotamian city. Ninevah was the home of a massive library, full of clay tablets written in **cuneiform**, the site of a temple dedicated to Nabu, the God of Writing. My parents love history, and I travel with them sometimes and have seen some incredible places.

But hardly anyone ever cared about that part of me, or my name. In fact, hardly anyone at school ever pronounced my name correctly, including some teachers, so I let them shorten it to Nine, which became Nines. And of course, when someone mispronounced a name in our class, everyone laughed and a new chance was born for someone to blow up the whole day. That's what we did. Our class was the worst that our school had ever seen.

It wasn't that we were bad kids. It was just a bad mix. There were smart kids, and not-so-smart ones, mixed in with loud ones and quiet ones of all different shapes and sizes. In fact, I read once that seventh graders can range from very, very small, to unusually large and well developed, and our class had all of that and more. It's the nature of the age to be, well, not normal. Our test scores were all over the charts, too, up and down, with no rhyme or reason. Elliot told everyone that low test scores got teachers in trouble and made their jobs harder, so a lot of the boys failed the state tests on purpose. On state testing day, they had to call in extra teachers to make sure the school did not fall out of compliance because of our behaviors. Teachers stood over us, breathing down our necks to make sure we were quiet and filled in all our bubbles. If they only knew how much they drove us crazy, maybe none of this would have had happened. We were always together, too, as one class, because that's how our school was – one small school, with one class for each grade. So we were together, year after year, starting in kindergarten and ending in eighth grade.

I was never bad; I just never talked. Teachers and subs tried to be nice to me about it, but I was sent out a lot, to the nurse or guidance counselors, especially when there was a blow-up in class and my anxiety kicked in. For two years, I didn't speak in school, because every time I did, I was made fun of, or corrected, or someone suggested something other than what I had said. So, I just gave up. I still spoke to my friends, and outside of school I was fine, but there was something about that school that bothered me. It wasn't fear; it was more like I felt *insulted* when nobody listened to me. I thought I was interesting, but apparently, teachers and some of my peers did not.

The whole time I was silent – from early fifth grade, until the seventh grade **exodus** – I wrote. I wrote what I thought, what I wanted to say, what other people said, and what happened. I kept my journal in the format of a newspaper, and called it *The Nines Observer*. Julian found it in my room once and thought it was great, so that's why I'm doing this now.

Not one teacher could control our awful class, except for Miss Robles, but she wasn't a teacher. She was a **therapist**. Yes, they had to call for outside help.

Therefore, we were not exactly surprised the night before the first day of school, when the mayor appeared on the five o'clock news and announced that this year, seventh grade is canceled.

Julian heard the news from the back seat of his mother's car. He had just come from karate class. They pulled up to the drive-through window just before the news came on the radio.

Julian always sat in the back seat of the BMW. Even though he was twelve, he was still very small for his age. Just to be safe, his parents made him ride in the back seat, on the passenger side because his Mom liked to be able to see him when she was driving.

He still remembers the smell of French fries that day in the car. Julian loves fries more than any other food. Ketchup or no ketchup, he doesn't care. The car smelled heavenly.

As his mother pulled away from the drive-thru window, she asked, "You okay back there, honey?"

"Yeah," was Julian's response. He was wearing his **gi.** His Sensei would be disappointed in him, seeing him eat French fries while wearing his gi. The uniform should only be worn while practicing karate. But his Mom didn't seem to care.

He didn't wear his belt in public. He was embarrassed. By now, he should have made his way to a higher belt, but he simply never passed the tests. His mother tried to console him by saying that he just needed more practice, but he knew the truth. It was because he was so small.

His mother fiddled with the radio. Julian watched as his mother turned the knob as if trying to find something. She looked like she needed some help, so he asked, "What are you looking for?"

"Nothing, Honey!" she responded, looking back at him over her shoulder. "Just thought I'd put on the news."

Odd, Julian thought. *She never listens to the news.* He thought of telling his Dad about his mother's strange behavior, but for the moment, the hot, salty fries were enough to keep his mind occupied. There was nothing else on Earth that made Julian so happy.

His mother found a station on the radio playing local news. They talked about traffic and weather, and the mayor's announcement, which would be broadcast live at 5 o'clock.

Samantha was eating a veggie burger at the dinner table when she heard the news. Here's her memory…

Samantha jumped down the stairs towards the kitchen. In Samantha's left hand was her hairbrush, a purple plastic mess, entwined with knots of thin, yellow strings of hair, a statement of her dedication to keeping her long hair perfectly straight. In her right hand was her phone. It was always attached to her, somewhere.

She skidded into the kitchen and sat at her seat, the one facing the TV. Without thinking, she placed her hairbrush to the left of her plate as she checked her phone for messages.

"Sam!" shouted her mother, with eyes that could move a mountain.

Sam looked up at her as if to ask, *what now?*

"Sorry," Sam apologized as she removed her hairbrush from the table and placed it beside her on her chair. She clicked her phone to her shorts and dug into her food.

"Can you take me shopping later?" she asked her Mom. "I need things for school."

"I can't. Jim's coming over."

"Mom!" Sam shouted. "Tomorrow's the first day of school and all you care about is your boyfriend? What about me? What am I supposed to wear, or bring, or EAT? You're my mother. You're supposed to be in charge of those things!"

June listened calmly to Samantha's rant, because, for the first time, June knew that Sam was going to lose this battle.

"Calm down. Maybe we can all go together," her mother suggested.

"What, so I can follow the two of you around town, holding hands and ignoring me?" Sam's eyes began to swell with tears. "Never mind!" Sam yelled, standing up. She pushed her chair back and picked up her plate of food.

"Wait," her mother said patiently. "There's something I need to tell you."

"*Please* tell me you're not getting married again," Sam said sarcastically, and slumped back into her chair, prepared to listen.

"I'm not supposed to tell you this, but…" Her words were cut off as the news came on the TV. June grabbed the remote from the counter, and turned up the volume.

"Just listen," she told Sam, nodding at the TV.

A short man in a business suit appeared before a crowd at what looked like the entrance to Shadyside School. The words "Special Report" blinked on and off in the corner of the screen. The school's principal stood beside him, eyes darting left to right as if he was nervous.

The man in the suit began to speak.

"Good evening. Tonight I have an official announcement to make on behalf of the parents and teachers of Shadyside School."

Sam looked quickly at her mother and said, "What's going on? Isn't that the mayor? And that's my principal. What happened?"

Her mother said nothing.

"In response to the demands and concerns of the parents and teachers of Shadyside School, the board of education and city government have approved the proposal to cancel seventh grade. All seventh graders should report to school tomorrow morning at the south bus ramp – not north - and bring with you the items listed in the packets that each family has received. You will be attending an interim location…until you are able to return as eighth graders. Your parents and guardians will review the new procedures with you at this point. Thank you," he finished, and quickly walked away.

"What is he talking about? We're going to another school? What 'items' do I need to bring? You knew about this? Why didn't you tell me?" Samantha's eyes were huge. She felt a rush of energy – a combination of anger, and an incredible fear.

"I'm sorry, honey. There was nothing I could do. Everyone agreed that this would be for the best. And, honey, all the teachers quit – they had heard about your class from the sixth grade teachers, and they refused to come back. We were sworn to secrecy."

"You hate me? I'm not *normal?*" She wanted to run to her mother, but at that moment, standing in her own kitchen, she saw her mother as a traitor who had gone behind her back and wanted to get rid of her. She wanted to run to her room and slam the door, but first she needed to get her hands on the list of items. And second, she needed to call her friends. She looked down at the ground, held out her hand, and said to her mother slowly so as not to cry, "Just give me the list."

There was an envelope that had been sitting on the counter. This was all part of the plan. June handed it to Sam and said, "There's also a note for you inside, from Miss Robles."

Sam's heart froze. Miss Robles knew about this, too? Sam spent many hours in her office, especially on the days when her teachers kicked her out of class for being loud, or talking back, or having, as they said, "a bad attitude." All of her classmates were bad, for their own reasons. She was only doing what they all did every day. *I guess*, she realized now, *they finally had enough.*

"Why did you wait so long to tell me?" Sam blurted out, on the verge of tears.

Her mother looked at her with a guilty expression on her face and said, "We were sworn to secrecy."

Elliot never heard the news. He just showed up on the first day of school and saw the bus. That bus. We are all rolling our eyes right now, and Elliot, Mark and Brian just walked in, so I think we need to tell you about the bus.

2

The bus was metallic blue. It was parked just outside the cafeteria door, at the bus loop. The sharp sunlight that reflected off the cafeteria windows at Shadyside School made the bus look more like a rocket ship. There were no words on the bus, just numbers, as if no one wanted to be responsible for it once it left the parking lot.

A line of cars moved through the parent drop-off lane as teachers directed traffic. The teachers were wearing blue t-shirts with yellow smiley faces on the front that said, "Welcome back!" One teacher was wearing a furry orange cat suit. It was Mr. Forest, the band director. He stood at the intersection of the bus loop and parent pickup, holding a sign that read, "7th grade, that way." An arrow pointed towards the bus loop, where students were being unloaded and then directed to where they were supposed to go. The sixth and eighth graders walked towards the auditorium for first day of school orientation. Seventh graders went straight towards the big sign that read, "Seventh grade here". There they waited in line to walk through the metal detector.

Parents were not to go past the metal detector. They already knew this, of course, because the information packet was sent to them long before the first day of school. They had agreed to say their goodbyes "quickly and efficiently," which Principal McThorn had requested at the last seventh grade cancellation meeting. At the front of the line was a small table where teachers were removing things that the students couldn't bring. As the parents left, they seemed to be juggling a load of contraband items: computers, iPhones, an electric guitar (it was Brian's Stratocaster). One parent was carrying a telescope back to the car.

I arrived at the end of the line with my suitcase. My brother dropped me off and then drove off to the high school. My parents were okay letting me go. We were scheduled to return for Christmas break. They bought me a new backpack, designed for camping and hiking. They said it will be great when we go on our next family adventure together.

I was okay with leaving. I certainly didn't want to return to another year of the mess they call school. I've always loved to travel. In fact, I never have anxiety attacks when I am traveling, just when I'm trapped at school.

Something about freedom appeals to me, and I get lots of new material for my newspaper when I'm on the road.

It didn't take long for the drama to start. Nicky was in the line, screaming. Her mother was there, shaking her head back and forth, and saying, "Nicky, say goodbye. I'm leaving and you can't come with me. If you don't say goodbye, you'll be sorry later. I'm saying goodbye. Nicky, say goodbye!"

It was a little scary, and made me uncomfortable.

Julian arrived just then, and stood behind me.

"Hi Nines," he said to me.

"Hi," I answered, and he gave me a little smile, which I understood to mean, *Cool, you're talking.*

"Why is there a metal detector here?" He asked his mother cautiously. She stayed with him in line to make sure he got through.

"It's just there to check for any electronic equipment," she replied. "I told you last night, no one's allowed to bring electronics from home. But you'll have everything you need once you get there, so don't worry."

I noticed his mother was actually smiling. She wasn't concerned about leaving Julian at Shadyside at all. The mayor and the principal promised the parents that this would be an amazing year for the seventh grade. All of the parents were excited for their kids to participate in this experience, which teachers and administrators called "positive" and "enriching."

"Where are we going?" Julian asked, stopping dead in his tracks when he saw the metallic blue bus.

"I can't tell you, you know that," his mother answered, and continued walking through the line, which was growing longer every minute. What she did not reveal to him was that she did not know where he was going.

The travel plans had been arranged by the Seventh Grade Cancellation Committee. Parents were not allowed to know exactly where the new school was located, to prevent "emotional reactions," as the committee called them. They assured the parents that it was all for the best, and that their new school would soon become the top school in the country for seventh grade.

Shadyside was a small mountain town, and their community was formed around a military base that specialized in high-level intelligence concerns. The families were all very different, yet they all shared two things common: they lived in this beautiful mountain town, and they all wanted a good education for their kids.

They knew the class caused a little bit of trouble, but the kids were fine at home, so parents assumed that the behavior problems were caused by the teachers. The Seventh Grade Enrichment Program sounded better than another year of detentions and parent teacher conferences.

Nicky finally began to quiet down. She stood facing away from her mother, who was talking on the phone. Nicky's eyes were watery. Her straight, brown bangs were glued to her forehead, damp with tears and sweat. She stared blankly, through her watery eyes, at the crowd of sixth and eighth graders headed toward the school building for the first day of school. She rubbed the end of her runny nose with the sleeve of her pink and purple striped sweater, and let out a hopeless sob.

She looked up at Julian from her place in line, wiped her nose with the other side of her sweater, and with a big sniff said, "Hi, Julian."

"Hi," Julian said, uneasily.

The line started moving. We all made it through the metal detector.

There was only one seventh grader who almost didn't make it through: Elliot.

Elliot and Samantha arrived at the same time. Sam was arguing with her mother, through her own tears. She wanted to blame her mother for all of her pain, but at the same time, she wanted her mother to rescue her from what she was about to go through. As she walked away from her mother, she heard a man's voice call out to her.

"Sam!" It was her Dad.

She dropped her bags and ran towards her father's car. He had parked illegally on the grass to avoid the parent pick-up line. His girlfriend Susan got out of the car.

Samantha squeezed her father tight.

"Daddy. You have to help me," she cried, tears rolling freely down her face.

"Sam, I tried to get you out of this, but there's nothing I can do. Nobody told me until last night!"

Sam sobbed into her father's shirt.

"Listen, honey. You are going to be fine. I will keep track of every step you take. I'm sorry I didn't see this coming, but now that I know, I will be there for you if anything happens. Okay?"

"I guess so," Sam said.

Susan walked over and said, "Good luck, Sam. We'll be here for you if you need us."

Sam pulled away from her Dad, wiping her tears and said, "Thanks."

She picked up her bags and walked back to the line. Her mother was there, and they said a quick goodbye. To Sam, it was all like a dream. Her parents were letting her go; she trusted them. So she went with the flow, knowing deep inside that sometimes she knew more about the truth than her parents ever did.

After saying goodbye to her mother, she got in line behind Elliot. Elliot walked through the metal detector and set off the alarm. They pulled him aside, and took away his survival kit. Julian and I heard the alarm go off, and turned to watch the scene.

"No! Give it back to me! That's mine!" Elliot carried his survival kit with him everywhere he went. He demanded to have it returned to him.

Unfortunately, Elliot had a history of discipline problems at the school. Everyone thought of him as trouble. The kit contained knives, and so they told him he could not take it with him.

"You're sending me into God knows where and you won't even let me bring my own personal belongings? What is this, the **Holocaust**?"

The security guard called into her walkie-talkie asking for assistance. Meanwhile, Samantha was ready to jump in.

"He needs his survival kit!" She yelled at the security guard. "You can't take it away from him!" She began moving toward the guard, grabbing for the blue bag.

The security guard held the survival kit above her head, as if playing keep away. Samantha and Elliot were restrained by teachers who had signed on for extra pay to help with the seventh grade switch.

Finally, Mr. Crane, the Assistant Principal, arrived.

"Thank God," Elliot said. "Someone half-way normal."

Mr. Crane was talking into his walkie as he arrived at the scene.

"Just take the knives out," he said to the security guards.

They looked at him as if he had two heads.

He rolled his eyes and grabbed for the blue bag.

"Give it to me," he said, and snatched it from their hands.

He took out the knives, and then handed the bag back to Elliot.

"I'll keep these safe until you come back. You can't take them with you, and you know why." Mr. Crane was friends with Elliot's Dad. They had been hunting together.

"Okay," Elliot agreed. He knew that weapons were not allowed at school, but he wasn't expecting a metal detector in the parking lot.

"I guess you can tell my Dad where I am," Elliot said to Mr. Crane.

Mr. Crane put a firm hand on Elliot's shoulder and said, "I will, and we'll be sending you all the supplies you'll need. You're going to have a great time, son. I think you'll be happier this year than I've seen you in the past. Now go," he said, and pointed towards the crowd of seventh graders seated in their assigned folding chairs at the loading dock, waiting to get on the bus.

The teachers loaded each seventh grader onto the bus like cruise directors introducing us to a luxury ship. Each student had a seat with their name on it, placed in alphabetical order. Each seat was equipped with a flat screen TV, packed with all the latest and greatest games and graphics. More giant flat screens lined the walls of the bus. Any of us, at any time, could choose a movie from the digital list and watch it with our friends, or alone, wearing headphones. Food was everywhere. Snacks spilled out of baskets beside every seat. Candy, cookies, donuts and fruit roll-ups were almost part of the decoration. In the back of the bus was a small area that looked like a kitchen with a bathroom. There was a freezer full of microwaveable food. The fridge was stocked with soda and juice.

The experience was very mesmerizing. It was like an arcade – flat screen televisions all around, with different movies and games – some of them connected to other kids, going on at the same time. It was everything a seventh grader could want. Soon everyone was in their seats, and the bus began to pull away, but we could hardly feel it moving…everyone was caught up in their own TV, DVD, and video game worlds.

Julian's seat was next to mine, in the middle, on the aisle. I was glad it was him, and not someone obnoxious.

He sat down next to me as I took out my journal and began to write, pretending to be a journalist on assignment for National Geographic.

"Nines?" Julian asked me. "Are you gonna talk this year?"

I laughed, "I will, unless someone freaks me out. I hope the teachers are nice there. Maybe they'll be cool, and things will be different."

"I hope so," he said. I saw Julian's eyes scan the ceiling of the bus, and take in all the sights and sounds. Julian was very observant. He noticed things – saw things that not everyone else could see. This was hard sometimes because he felt like he was not normal. Now, on the bus, he saw something that he couldn't believe no one else had noticed. At first, he felt a kick in his stomach. Then, he felt a bizarre sense that this was okay. Eventually, the reality came to him when he cleared his thoughts and really took a good look around him. What Julian realized was that no one was driving the bus.

Nicky was still crying. At this point, her striped sweater was sopping wet, her eyes swollen and red. Her sobs were slowing down, though, and it was clear that she might not have any energy left to keep up the sobbing noises. She curled back into her chair and stared at Samantha's screen. Sam, seated next to her because their last names both started with T, was watching a movie with headphones. Nicky just sort of laid back and stared at the silent screen, exhausted from the crying and the emotional shock of being ripped from her parents and her home.

"Feeling better?" Samantha asked Nicky.

"Mph," Nicky puffed through her sweater, which covered her mouth and nose.

"I'm sure we'll be fine," Sam said to make Nicky feel better.

"Mph," Nicky said, and soon fell asleep sitting up in her seat.

I was sitting next to Julian, and I could feel his mind racing. He was still trying to figure out who was driving the bus. We had been on the road for thirty minutes. Where was the driver? What was going on?

As if he could read Julian's mind, Elliot looked backwards from his seat in the front row (his last name starts with an A). He saw Julian sitting near me. Elliot trusted Julian. They had been in many classes together, but their houses were very far away from each other, so they didn't hang out much after school. Elliot lived at the national forest, where his father was the park ranger, and Julian's father was a doctor so he lived closer to town.

They made eye contact. Elliot had already figured it out. No driver. Too many toys. Junk food. They were distracting us. They didn't want us to think about the truth – the moment, what was real. They were using everything they could think of to hypnotize us into believing that everything was okay, so that we didn't react, didn't freak out the way we did in class. They were trying to outsmart us.

On the keyboard at his seat, Julian saw a link that the seventh graders could use for instant messaging on board the bus. He decided to send Elliot a message. He wrote: "Hey, man. Who's driving the bus?"

Elliot wrote back, smiling: "No clue, dude. Any ideas?"

Julian wrote back: "Are they trying to kill us?"

And Elliot replied: "No way, man, that's illegal. But there's something going on. And, they are probably reading everything we write. Let's stay on top of it. Deal?"

Julian wrote: "Deal. Hey, do you know how to drive a bus?"

Elliot wrote back: "Totally man. No worries," and then thought to himself, *if it has a steering wheel, gas pedal and brakes.*

Elliot knew how to drive. Living in national forests had its benefits. He and his dad always lived in remote locations, far from anyone else. His father taught him to drive at a young age. He wanted to make sure Elliot could take care of himself, in any situation. Since his father drove the park vehicles, Elliot had many chances to drive their old Bronco through the dirt roads in the park, and he helped his dad work on cars sometimes, too.

We were on that bus for hours, and it wasn't long before the conflicts began to arise. We were, after all, the famous class that teachers dreaded every year, the group that always got into trouble, the kids banned from field trips, movies, even parties, as we watched the other kids in the school enjoy their rewards.

Some special cases added variety to the mix, like Tanya, for example. Tanya has a special condition where she can't control the volume of her voice. She has a doctor's note for it, and the teachers have to make accommodations for her. Tanya always yells. She yells at kids, teachers, herself. She screams when she is happy, sad, angry and confused. All day, before, during and after school, Tanya's voice would ring throughout the school, spreading across the soccer field, through the cafeteria, and bouncing back and forth on the walls of the classroom. In fact, Tanya is probably the number one reason why I am so good at reading and writing, because the teachers used to send me to the library when Tanya went haywire so I wouldn't go into a panic attack.

Most people yell back at Tanya when she yells at them. Our teachers begged us, "Please, just ignore her." But, who can ignore someone yelling in your face? So someone would always yell back, and a fight would start, and everyone would get involved. Eventually Tanya would get tired out because yelling took a lot of energy. She would calm down, look around at everyone, smile, and say, "I love you guys." Then everyone would sigh with relief, knowing Tanya was done for the day.

So it was no surprise that she was standing up on top of her seat, the last seat in the back, since her last name starts with a Z. Her mouth was wide open, screaming a frightening list of words at Brian Watts, who was sitting in the seat in front of her, and was mad at her for yelling in his ear.

"Don't you tell me what to do!" Tanya wailed. "You don't even know what you're talking about!"

Brian was very patient, and did not want to start a fight. He knew there was nothing he could say to shut her up, so he took deep breaths and tried to say nothing at all. He prayed that she wouldn't get physical. He'd seen her yank a clump out of Nicky's hair once. He thought to himself, *Just wait a little longer, and she'll cave.*

But even though our class had been through this before, there was something different now. Now there were no adults to protect her. Everyone was stressed to their limits, having been through a very traumatic morning, and eating gobs of junk food that had no nutritional value. Everyone's nerves were fried.

A large boy in the middle row stood up. It was Mark. Mark had stayed back in third grade because he failed the reading test. He was older, and stronger, and liked to be a bully. He stood up very slowly, turned his big, doublewide body sideways, looked Tanya straight in the eyes, and said, threateningly, "Will you SHUT UP?"

"Oh, great. Here we go," Elliot mumbled, and looked back at Julian. He hoped this didn't turn into a rumble. If it did, he decided he'd try to protect Julian from the other kids, because Julian was so small, and Elliot thought he was a cool kid. He looked over at Samantha, too. Sam and Elliot knew each other pretty well. They went to summer camp together at the national forest where Elliot lived. Her eyes met his and she gave him her classic eye roll, which meant, "Can you believe this?"

Tanya lost it. She jumped over the seat in front of her, kicking Brian in the face and leaving a sneaker print on his T-shirt. Mark tried to make a run for it, but there was nowhere to go. The smaller kids tried to hide from them, and big kids tried to get between them, but Tanya eventually caught up to Mark, and grabbed his hair with her two bony hands.

"OW!" Mark screamed, grabbed Tanya by the waist, and lifted her over his head, shaking her upside down until she let go of his hair.

"STOP IT! I'M GONNA PUKE!" Tanya screamed. She was beginning to lose her voice. It was starting to crackle.

"Someone needs to teach you a lesson," Mark said, looking up at her from down below. "No one's gonna put up with your garbage here."

Just then, a funny expression came over Tanya's face. She opened her mouth, but this time what came out was not noise, but gallons of root beer and green gummy bears.

The entire class started screaming. People near the puke pile tried to get away. Those who looked around for a window to open suddenly realized there was none; TV screens had replaced them. The reality of the situation started to hit everyone this time. Soon other kids were throwing up from motion sickness, fear and all of the nasty smells around them.

Then suddenly, the bus came to a smooth, slow stop. Everybody froze. A feeling of relief buzzed through the mobile room. Hope seemed to arrive. All eyes turned to the door, expecting it to open.

But it didn't. Instead, the TV screens, which surrounded the inside of the bus where the windows should have been, all tuned into the same image. It was Principal McThorn!

Shock, more than anything, kept everyone quiet. We listened carefully as he spoke.

"Well, students, once again I see that you have put yourselves in a sticky mess," he laughed, happy that he was not there with us in the stinky confinement of the bus.

"You know, this situation could have easily been avoided if you had just used your anger management strategies – the ones I have taught you, year after year, to help you learn to be kinder and gentler people."

Kids shifted in their seats, listening.

"I suppose I should take this opportunity to explain to you where you are, and what you will be learning at your new Seventh Grade Enrichment Camp. You will all be staying at a state of the art facility, equipped with the most advanced technology available to schools. In fact, some of it is still in the experimental stage, and you kids will be the first to test it! Be proud to know that you will be learning with equipment provided to our school by such groups as NASA and the National Intelligence Agency! Your job is to follow the protocol, which will be explained to you when you arrive, and soon you will be ready to return to Shadyside and share your knowledge with your parents and fellow students. Our goal is to make you into good citizens who respect their school, and can follow the rules we have in place for your safety and learning. Let's be honest, kids: nothing else has worked. Your teachers and administrators have done everything they can. Now it's up to you. When the doors open, you will see a sign to follow. Take your bags from the luggage compartment below, and stay together! I'm sorry there are no adults here to help you, but that is part of the enrichment. Actually, we couldn't find anyone who was willing to go with you. Remember, you are not alone. We are monitoring you very closely, and we can be there if you *truly* need our help."

Then the screens flickered off and the bus door slid open with a swoosh. Fresh air entered the bus, and everyone scrambled to get out.

Elliot, who was way in the front, turned to the kids in the back and yelled, "Grab some food from the kitchen!" A bittersweet happiness returned to the seventh graders. We were thrilled to get off the bus and see our new school!

3

The bus had stopped at the end of a dirt road, leaving a cloud of fumes that smelled like rotten eggs. The seventh grade stood together, holding our backpacks and suitcases. A sign, made of cheap plywood and black spray paint, was nailed to a tree on the other side of the road. It said, "7th Grade THAT WAY" with an arrow pointing towards a narrow dirt path.

We were in the middle of nowhere. The only sounds we heard were the sounds we made ourselves, diffused by a gentle wind that blew softly. It was a beautiful day, but I began to feel my anxiety creeping up on me from deep inside. I had the realization that we were abandoned. Ahead of us was nothing but a small path through the woods, and behind us, a rocky dirt road lined by trees. If anything happened, who would know? Who would come to save us?

"Nines, let's stay close to Elliot," Julian said to me after we got our bags. For some reason, we felt safer being near the forest ranger's son. We walked around a group of girls and stood next to Elliot.

"So, what do you think of this?" Julian asked him.

"To be honest with you, I don't know what to think right now," Elliot answered.

The luggage had been handed out, and the group stood, waiting for some kind of sign that we should go. As if someone had heard our thoughts, the bus's engine started up again, the door and luggage compartment slid closed, and the bus began to pull away. Julian and Elliot looked at each other and shook their heads.

They watched as the bus backed up and turned down the road.

"I looked," Julian told Elliot. "There's no way there could have been someone in there."

"NASA," Elliot said. Nothing surprised him anymore.

Samantha and Nicky showed up next to us. We all felt safe with Elliot.

"I guess we should start walking," Sam said, her eyes scouting out the path ahead.

"I guess we should," Elliot decided, and bravely led the seventh grade into the wilderness.

We walked mostly in silence for the first twenty minutes, lugging baggage and taking in the surroundings. Tanya's voice was completely gone, which was a blessing that no one overlooked. We were in the mountains, and the path led us first through a grassy meadow, then narrowed into a cool, leafy forest of trees, and finally out to a rocky lookout point where we could see for miles.

"Where are we going?" I asked.

Everyone looked at each other, hoping somebody would have an idea.

"We're pretty high in the mountains," Elliot said.

"What's all that smoke?" I wondered.

"It's just clouds," Elliot explained. "They're lower than the mountaintops."

The group reassembled at the lookout point. Everyone sat down and took a break, eating snacks we saved from the bus, and checking up on each other to make sure we had not lost anyone. We had been walking for two hours.

Mark came up from the trail, carrying Nicky on his back. She was exhausted, and looked sad and forlorn, her head resting heavily on Mark's shoulder.

"What's the story?" He called out to Elliot.

"Well, we must be pretty close. They couldn't send us much farther than this. It would be too remote, and you can't have buildings that far from a road. It's just impossible." He was trying to sound hopeful, but he feared that his voice was showing the truth: that he was worried about nightfall.

"So we should just keep following the same path?" Mark asked him.

"Yes. Do not, under any circumstances, let anyone go off the path!" Elliot shouted with a serious tone.

Mark answered, "Got it."

We rested for a while, and then rounded the bend back into the forest. Soon, the path became wider. We followed it down past a waterfall stream, and into a clearing. There, in the distance, was our school.

It was a group of houses, all different sizes. It reminded Sam of the summer camp where she and Elliot had spent so many days. There were many dirt roads around it, which gave hope that we might be closer to civilization than we thought. It was Julian who made the connection first, always thinking like a spy. He picked up his feet and shuffled up over a few roots and boulders to catch up with Elliot.

"It was another distraction," he wheezed to Elliot's shoulder. His asthma was kicking in, and he wasn't used to the strenuous exercise.

Elliot turned his head and looked down at Julian questioningly.

"The trail. They want us to think we're farther away than we really are."

"You are so right. Good thinking!" Elliot replied, and the two boys sped up to get a closer look at their new home.

Sam squinted to read a crooked wooden sign nailed to a fence. It said, "Sunnyside Farms."

Brian was behind her. He said, "It looks like an abandoned campground or something."

The buildings were made of wood and stone, probably taken from the forests surrounding them. There were big glass windows, and one building had a deck that stretched out of what must have been the dining hall, filled with circular tables and chairs.

The seventh graders had all arrived, and were roaming in and out of the buildings, which were rustic, but not too old. All of the doors were unlocked. It was clean, and everything worked. It was obvious that people had been there recently to get the school ready for us.

It was Mark who finally stepped out into the central courtyard and shouted what we had all started to notice.

"There's no adults here!" he shouted with joy. "We're FREE!" He did a little dance, and a few of the boys ran over to give him a big high five. The boys outnumbered the girls three to one. That is one of the reasons our class was so completely annoying.

At first, I didn't believe we were alone. I was sure that the adults were here somewhere, in the office. Or perhaps they had gone into town for supplies, and we arrived earlier than expected. But I was wrong. We were completely alone, on top of a mountain, in the middle of the forest.

Everyone broke out to explore the grounds, and find places to stay. There were two buildings filled with dorm rooms. The beds were made, bathrooms stocked with supplies. It was sort of like a hotel.

Most of the girls chose to stay in the Holly House, which had a big center room equipped with a huge TV, and bright, pretty bathrooms. The boys were happier in the Lookout Lodge, because it was decorated with a hunting theme, and giant stuffed deer heads lined the halls.

Samantha put her things in one of the rooms. She was sharing a room with me. She didn't really want to stay so closely tied to all of the other girls; they were just too catty for her. They talked about things that were meaningless, like gossip or rumors. She slipped away to explore the camp on her own while I was unpacking. She was starving.

She went straight to the dining hall. It was a big, open room filled with round tables and plastic chairs. In the back was the kitchen. Sam was dying to see what there was to eat.

The kitchen looked like any other restaurant kitchen. There was a walk-in refrigerator, giant stoves, and a dishwashing line set up to handle a crowd. She walked through the kitchen, looking up at the pots and pans, and eyeing the knife rack, which she noticed was empty. She suddenly felt the urge to find a knife for Elliot. She knew how upset he was that he couldn't bring the ones in his survival kit. She rummaged through the utility drawers, hoping to find some kind of sharp kitchen tool. Nothing.

The sharpest thing in that kitchen was a butter knife. She took one anyway.

Finally, she looked closely at the food. There was fruit, apples and bananas, eggs, bread, cereal and milk for the mornings, frozen pizza, hamburgers, hot dogs and ice cream, a few frozen dinners, and some things for kids with certain dietary restrictions. That was it. Sam felt a knot in the pit of her stomach. She didn't want anything here. They had taken away her family, her friends who were back in eighth grade, her phone, her things, and now they were taking food out of her mouth! She felt overwhelmed. She wasn't sure if she could take it anymore. She wondered exactly how to get in touch with the principal, send him a message that she was having an emergency. She looked around for a camera or something, anything that might be a way for them to see her, but she did not see anything.

She sat on the kitchen floor, her hand grasping the handle of the butter knife, and began to cry.

Sam sat that way for at least ten minutes, feeling miserable, and hoping that someone, somewhere was watching her, and would see that she really needed help right now.

She sat up when she heard a loud noise in the dining area. The double doors opened with a bang, and in marched half of the entire population of the Lookout Lodge. *The boys*, she thought, and rolled her eyes to no one. She wiped her nose with her sleeve, pushed herself up off the floor, and walked quickly out of the kitchen.

A line of boys passed her on her way out, all of them smiling as if they had just won the lottery.

"You cooking dinner, Sam?" Mark snickered as she walked past.

"Not for you," she answered, and headed towards the door.

"Hey, Sam," Brian called out, and touched her sleeve. "Have you seen Elliot? Where is he now?"

Sam shrugged. "I dunno. What do I look like, his keeper?"

"No, silly. I'm just concerned is all. No one's seen him in about an hour, and we want to have a meeting in the Lodge tonight. If you see him, will you tell him?"

"Sure," Sam assured him, and headed outside. She knew where he was, of course. If she knew him, which she did, he was walking the perimeter of the camp, looking for a way out.

The year his Mom died was the year that Elliot's behavior problems started. He started hating grownups, doing everything he could to prove that they were stupid and that nobody had any idea what they were talking about. To him, nothing really mattered anymore. He was always angry, angry at the world for being so cruel.

One day, Miss Handler was teaching the class about the circulatory system. She was explaining how the heart works, and saying that today, modern medicine can heal almost anything.

"That's not true. Why don't you shut up, you stupid frogface," Elliot blurted out from the back of the room.

Miss Handler was stunned. She picked up the telephone and dialed the office. Soon someone arrived to escort Elliot out. They placed him in a small storage room, which was a makeshift office, to wait for the principal, because, apparently, Principal McThorn was very busy in his real office dealing with another issue, and there was a line of kids in the waiting area. The window in the little room was open, and Elliot could feel the cool breeze of the outside world coming in. He wanted to get out of there, out of the prison they called school, but the hinges on the window were designed to keep it from opening all the way out. A safety feature, he laughed. He sat and stared, waiting for the principal to come and sentence him to the latest punishment. Then, something came over him. He needed to escape, get away from this suffocating world of people who didn't understand him. He looked through the drawers of the desk in the room and found a small metal staple remover. It fit perfectly into the screws that held the window hinges in place. Within five minutes, Elliot was walking down the street towards the Taco Bell.

4

Sam was tired, and she didn't think Elliot could ever need her help. He was so strong. He could do things she never could do, like sleep in the wilderness, face wild animals, or…live without a Mom.

She walked back to the dorm room where she had left her things, and no one was there; the girls had gone down to the dining hall. She sat on the bed. *There's nothing for me here,* she thought, yet had trouble knowing the difference between her thoughts and her feelings. *Elliot would know what I need,* she decided. She fished through her suitcase, found her hiking boots, threw them on her feet, and walked outside to go looking for him.

It was still light when Elliot set out to identify their location. It was a beautiful spot, the kind of place anyone would want to live. Thick forests surrounded them. Granite boulders enhanced the gorgeous lookout points where one could see for miles. The land was farmable in the warm months, and full of minerals to sell if you knew how to mine them.

Not many people lived this high up for two main reasons: one, because the roads closed as soon as the temperature hit freezing, and two, because once the roads closed, you had no way of getting off the mountain. Most of the buildings at Camp Sunnyside were designed for warm-weather visitors. Elliot knew very well that this "camp" the principal had sent them to could not support them through the cold winter months in the mountains.

He traced the dirt road trails in his mind, walking and thinking. He would follow them down the hill tomorrow. His mind was racing. He was glad that Julian was on his side. He walked, contemplatively, for about two miles, taking everything in. He circled the entire camp but did not find a road, just a series of wide paths that led nowhere.

By the time that Elliot was back at the camp, the sun was beginning to set across the mountains, and the dining hall was being blown out to kingdom come.

Sam found a path that curved around the back of Lookout Lodge, with wooden steps leading to a trail, designed for walking. She followed it, absorbing the handcrafted woodwork, made from branches from this very forest. At the end of the wooden boardwalk, through a thick forest of trees, was another building no one else had discovered. Samantha walked into the unlocked doorway, confident that no one was there, because at that point almost everyone else was in the kitchen, pigging out on pizza and ice cream.

The wooden door squeaked when she opened it, and a musty smell of moss and wildflowers filled her nose. A stone foyer and a table full of dried flowers is what she first saw. Around the corner was an entrance to a big room, with a raised stage in the front, all covered by a beige rug. Samantha recognized this as some kind of religious place. People came here to pray, she knew. She took off her boots and walked to the front of the room.

For some reason, Samantha had a feeling that the people who used to live here had to leave unexpectedly. She couldn't tell exactly why or how she knew, but it just made sense to her that this place was not dead; it was simply being rented out.

Sam was comfortable with spiritual things. Her Mom was an astrologer, so things like that were always second nature to her. She walked up to the stage and kneeled down. She placed the butter knife on the rug, and began to pray.

Dear God, I'm sorry for whatever I did to make everyone hate me. Please tell my parents and my teachers that I will do whatever it takes to make them accept me again. I guess I did something wrong; God, please tell me what I did wrong so I can fix it. I didn't mean to hurt anyone. And tell my dog Star that I miss her and love her. Sam.

And that's when she heard the fire alarm.

The boys had quickly destroyed the kitchen, cooking most of the pizzas in the giant ovens, and eating ice cream straight from the containers. In all truth, they didn't know any better; most of them never had to cook and clean at home. They were kids, and their parents took care of those things. Most of the girls showed up, and found things to eat, too. A group of boys took a crate of eggs and climbed up the old oak tree outside the dining hall. They were throwing eggs at squirrels, birds, and anyone who walked beneath the tree.

Then, at exactly 6 o'clock, a voice was heard over what seemed to be an intercom.

"May I have your attention, please, seventh graders." Everyone stopped eating and looked up, wondering where the voice was coming from.

"It's McThorn." Mark huffed, and everyone froze.

"Welcome to your new home, students. I see you have found some dinner. Please feel free to order more food from the computer lab, which is set up in the office of Community Hall. I am very proud of you for making it so far. Keep up the good work. For now, enjoy yourselves and get some sleep tonight. It has been a long day. Tomorrow morning at 9 a.m., please report to the Community Hall computer lab, and log into the computers for your first day of classes. The log-in codes are the same as last year. Once you log in, you will be able to communicate directly with myself and Jason, your web-based teacher. The computers are only able to access the special intranet we have designed for you, not the internet. If you need to send a message to your parents, simply send it to Jason, and he will deliver it to them immediately. You're doing great, seventh grade. Keep up the good work!"

And then it was silent.

Everyone looked at each other, wondering what to say. Finally, Mark broke the ice and said, "I'm goin' to the computer lab!" He took off running towards the front door. Suddenly, everyone saw the magic in his idea. *We can contact our parents*, they thought, *send a message to someone out there…order new food.* Everyone who was in the kitchen made a run for the door, leaving half-eaten pizza crusts and open ice cream containers all over the counters. The ovens were still on, blazing hot. And someone, no one will ever know who, left a pizza box on top of the gas oven.

When we reached the computer lab, we were met with a locked door. Mark grabbed the door handle and shook it, trying to get it open.

There was a sign on the door, in the glass. Tanya read it out loud so everyone could hear.

"Computer Lab hours: 8 a.m. to 6 p.m. Door will be opened and locked automatically at these times."

"What time is it?" Someone shouted.

"6:05." Tanya said, looking at her watch.

Another disappointment loomed over us, and we walked wearily back towards the Lodge, hoping to find entertainment in the movies and video games.

And then the fire alarm went off. It blared across campus, throughout every room. Someone yelled, "The kitchen!"

Black smoke burst out of the kitchen window. Brian, Mark and three other boys ran around back to the kitchen door.

"Is this a good idea?" Brian asked before they went inside. He knew that firefighters died all the time from inhaling smoke. He had no idea how to fight a fire.

"It's small," Mark said, panting from running so fast. "There are extinguishers near every stove. Grab one!" And the boys stormed in to put out the blaze.

Apparently, there was a sprinkler system installed in the kitchen. It went off just as the boys entered the smoky room. White powdery foam that smelled like chemicals sprayed onto the stoves, and Mark sprayed down the rest of the smoldering pizza box with a hand-held extinguisher.

The stovetop fire was stopped before it got out of hand. The window near the stove was blown out and the walls and stove were black. The entire kitchen was now covered in a blanket of white foam. But everyone was okay.

Slowly, the others came in from the back door as well as through the front doors of the dining hall. Feet sloshed through the foam, which covered most of the kitchen floors. Mark leaned against the counter and rubbed his forehead with the back of his hand. He looked over at Brian, and held his hand out for a shake, saying "Thanks, dude."

When Tanya walked in, her shrieks broke the solemn mood.

A noise came out of her that sounded like an animal, definitely not human.

Everyone covered their ears, and when she was done, Mark said to Tanya, "Someone said you started the fire." He smiled viciously. He couldn't help it. Something in him just wanted justice done.

"What? You know you started it, so you better just shut up before I…" Tanya had to stop talking then, because Mark and Brian, in hero mode, took off running.

Around 6:30 p.m., the message was relayed from person to person for everyone to meet at Lookout Lodge. It was the biggest building in the camp, and had a giant room with high ceilings, big couches, and lots of chairs where everyone could sit comfortably together and talk. Brian found an old cowbell on the fireplace and started to ring it outside, calling out, "TOWN MEETING! LOOKOUT LODGE! COME 'N GET IT!" over and over again.

Eventually, everyone arrived. The boys had set up all the televisions they could find around the perimeter of the central room. Movies and video games were playing non-stop. It was like a game room. They found board games and set them up on the tables. Sports equipment was brought in from the closets of Community Hall, and footballs and basketballs were streaming through the air. Two of the boys had brought a whole pizza back to their room before the fire, and were eating it on the couch. Some of the girls brought a tub of ice cream over from the kitchen and were laughing and eating at the same time.

For the most part, everyone was fine. There never was a town meeting that night. It was more like a party.

Elliot sat outside on the porch, listening to the night critters and looking at the stars. Sam found him there and sat down next to him.

"Where were you all day?" she asked him.

"I walked down the road a little, looked around to see what's here," he said.

"And what did you find?" Samantha asked.

"Nothing," he answered, and the two of them sat in silence, gazing off into the dark night.

5

The next morning, Julian woke up on the floor in front of the living room TV. Brian was lying there beside him, the remote control still in his right hand, his mouth wide open in deep sleep. The moose head clock on the stone wall said 8:30 a.m. Julian remembered the principal's message from the night before. Their first class started at 9 o'clock in the computer lab.

He raced to his room to put on some clothes, waking people up as he sped by them. There were girls sleeping in sleeping bags on the floor of the great room. They had been afraid to walk to the Holly House in the dark. They woke up as he sped by complaining that he was being too loud.

Julian shared a room with V.J., who was already awake. They agreed to walk to class together. They stopped in the Dining Hall on the way there, half expecting a hot breakfast to be ready and waiting for them. But all they found was the same dirty kitchen with white foam, dirty dishes and empty food containers scattered everywhere.

They salvaged a box of cereal, two bowls, spoons, and milk, and ate breakfast at one of the round dining tables.

"How come no one else is up?" Julian asked V.J.

"Because they don't care," V.J. said. "Look who we're dealing with. Most of our class never cared about their grades. Half of them hate reading altogether. I'm sort of glad that they have a choice now, because I can finally learn something without having to sit there while some kid disrupts the entire day."

Julian agreed with V.J. It was hard to be the good kid when you were surrounded by bad kids. Yeah, they were all friends because they'd known each other so long, but that didn't mean they had to like each other.

The boys finished eating and added their dirty dishes to the pile in the kitchen sink.

They were the first to arrive at the computer lab, and the doors opened easily. The computers were new, and they both logged in successfully. A message came up in bright, bold colors that read, "Good morning seventh grade. Your program will begin at 9 a.m. sharp. Please wait patiently." Some of the others started streaming in, including me and Nicky, but when 9 o'clock arrived, most of the seventh grade was still missing.

The program started. It began with an announcement, "Please place your headphones on your ears, then press Enter." Inside the headphones, Julian heard the voice of a friendly man, talking directly to him. The man introduced himself as Jason, the online instructor. Our new teacher. He said, "Good morning Julian. Thank you for making it to class on time. I have chosen some activities that I think you will enjoy so follow the prompts and begin. Your first assignment is to take the multiple-choice Reading Placement Test. Please try your best, and remember to read all of the choices before you select your answers. I have great faith in you. Good luck!"

Julian began the test. He liked to read, but he hoped it wasn't going to be too hard. Even though he was smart, he got anxiety during tests. He was always afraid that the questions would be too confusing for him, afraid that he would fail. And it didn't help that the passages they had to read were always so boring.

The first article was entitled, "Preventing Bear Attacks." It told of ways to stay away from bears, and said that if you found yourself face-to-face with a wild bear, the best thing to do is play dead. The next part talked about the kind of foods that bears ate. One of the things was dead animals.

Julian had to stop and re-read that part. *Wait a minute…*he thought. *Why is it okay to play dead if a bear eats dead animals? Wouldn't he think you were food?* He couldn't figure it out. A tight knot began building in the top of his stomach. Now not only was the article confusing, he still didn't know what he should do if he sees a bear. And Elliot had already told him that there are bears up on the mountain. He started feeling a strong desire to go home, and he missed his parents in a painful way.

The next article was called, "Foraging for Food in the Wild." It taught ways to figure out which foods are edible and which were poisonous, and had lists of edible plants and animals that he was told to memorize, as he would be quizzed on them later.

When he finished the placement test, a "Congratulations!" screen flashed up and Jason appeared on the screen.

"Great Job, Julian!" Jason said. "Now, click on the Intranet icon, and send a message to your folks back home!"

Julian felt a wave of relief and joy come over him. He found the message board, and started writing like wildfire, telling his mother and father everything that had happened to him so far, and begging them, using good spelling and grammar, to please, please, please, come and get him.

The students who arrived after 9 o'clock were unable to open the door to the computer lab. A robotic, female voice came on as they tried to turn the door handle stating, "Sorry. You are tardy. You will need to make up your work tomorrow. Please try to make it to class on time." They were left dumbfounded. The kids who decided to show up really just wanted to email their parents.

The seventh graders were hungry. A group of them was rifling through the kitchen trying to make some lunch, but it was impossible to see through the giant mess of dirty dishes, pizza boxes, and dried up white foam that was covering all of the countertops and rolling over onto the floor. Roaches had appeared everywhere, and the girls screeched when they saw them. Some of the girls – and boys - were so terrified by the roaches that they refused to go into the kitchen and said they'd rather starve than see those roaches ever again.

"What are we going to do about this mess?" Mark asked Brian.

Mark and Brian knew that they would have to take charge, but they had no idea how to get their classmates to chip in and help clean the kitchen. Mark knew that people would listen to him because he was the oldest, and the biggest. Brian felt like he needed to help, because he felt sad for the other kids who felt so helpless.

Finally, Brian remembered something the Principal had said to him after he'd gotten in trouble for starting a food fight. "Your behavior sets an example for others to follow."

"We'll clean it up, and make some dinner, then we won't let anyone have any food until they sign up for their kitchen duty time."

Mark looked at him for a minute. He didn't like the part when Brain said, "We'll clean up," but he knew it was the only way to get through this problem, and he didn't mind the work. After all, they had nothing else to do since they were locked out of the computer lab.

They got to work cleaning dishes, mopping the floor. It turned out to be sort of fun. While they cleaned, they brainstormed ideas for the big dinner they would cook, and the other items they would order from the central computer. Brian found some duct tape and a plastic tablecloth in the storage room, and used it to cover the broken window. Once the kitchen was clean, the roaches disappeared and went back into the wall and the ceiling and the other places where they live.

Finally, the boys brought out hot dogs and hamburgers, set up a serving line, and started to cook. Delicious smells wafted outside through the broken window in the back of the kitchen, and seventh graders began appearing at the kitchen door like lost puppies begging for scraps of food.

"Come on in!" Mark waved to everyone who showed up. "You can eat as soon as you sign this agreement." He handed a clipboard to the crowd, and no one dared to complain.

Elliot was about a mile west of the camp when he saw smoke drifting up from among the trees on the side of a hill. *Campfire*, he thought. *There's someone there.*

He veered off the dirt trail he had been following, and headed straight for that fire. Even though he made himself – and the class – a promise to never stray from the path alone, he felt that this was one of those times when he needed to break the rules. He took out a ball of string from his survival kit and let it fall on the ground behind him, a guide to help him find his way back to the trail.

He could smell the wood burning. Whoever had made the fire was not very good at it, because it was mostly smoke.

As he neared closer to the campsite, he heard footsteps, and the rustling of leaves. He stopped in his tracks. *This could be some serial killer hiding from the law*, he thought. He let a few minutes pass before he snuck behind a grove of wild rhododendron and peeked through the trees at a small clearing where someone had set up a tent and was hanging their laundry to dry on the branches of an oak tree. And that's when he saw her. Elliot's heart almost stopped for a full second. *It's Miss Robles*, he realized.

Samantha had been following Elliot all afternoon. After class was let out, she went looking for him, and saw him walking through a mountain stream collecting rocks. She didn't want him to be mad at her for looking for him, so she just sort of dragged behind far enough away so he wouldn't see her. Sam wanted to tell Elliot about the little church she had found, but she was afraid he would laugh at her. She still felt uneasy about telling him.

When he veered off the path, she knew something was up. Soon, she could smell the smoke, too. Finally, her curiosity became so intense that she forgot about her worries and walked right up behind Elliot, who was hiding behind a bunch of rhododendron bushes.

"Oh my gosh! Miss Robles!" she screamed, and ran bounding through the bushes towards the fire.

Miss Robles screamed in shock and fear, probably thinking she was being chased by a mountain lion or something. She jumped up and looked around for a place to hide, but gave up. Her cover was blown. She hugged Samantha and smiled.

"Hi Samantha. How are you?" She asked calmly.

"HOW AM I? How do you THINK I am? I've been kidnapped and stolen from my parents, left on the top of a mountain to die!" Tears started coming down her cheeks and soon she was sobbing into Miss Robles' khaki fishing vest, which was full of a variety of different camping tools.

"Oh, Sam, I know it seems hard, but you need to hang in there. You'll see. There's a great prize waiting for you at the end of this experience. Is that Elliot with you?" She asked, looking into the woods.

Elliot came out into eyeshot, walking slowly over to Miss Robles and Sam.

He said, "Why are you here?"

"I was worried about you," she said. "All of you."

Elliot was quick to respond, "Well, apparently, we are perfectly fine, and we have everything we could possibly need for our Seventh Grade Enrichment Experience. You had something to do with this, didn't you? Was it your idea to kill us off?" His eyes were wild with anger.

Miss Robles remained calm. She knew Elliot so well by now, and she knew he would not resort to violence, that his reactions came from a deep inner pain he had experienced when he lost his mother, and the new hurt that he felt when his father ignored him.

"No one is trying to kill anyone," she assured them both. "It wasn't my idea, all of this, but truthfully, I think it's a good thing. Your class never tried to change. School became a joke after third grade when the reading tests got harder and everyone learned that if someone was bad you wouldn't have to do work because the teachers would be distracted."

"You knew that?" Sam asked, and this time Miss Robles rolled her eyes. "Duh!" She said, and they laughed.

"Please don't tell anyone I'm here," she asked Samantha and Elliot. From the looks of her campsite, it looked like she was planning to stay for a while. She had a small Recreational Vehicle, or RV, with a little awning off the side, a table, and one chair. The tent was set up outside as an extra room.

The two students looked at each other and understood. They liked having an important secret, and they liked having an adult nearby that they could go to if they needed help. They liked the fact that Miss Robles cared enough about them to risk her life spying on them to make sure they were safe. Their eyes clicked, and they knew.

"Okay," Sam agreed, and for the first time in three days, she felt happy. "Can we bring you anything?"

Miss Robles nodded and said, "I could go for a burger and fries!"

They all laughed, and Sam and Elliot headed back to camp.

As they walked up the hill, Samantha and Elliot came up with a new plan. It was something the teachers and parents would never see coming.

6

Mark and Brian were tired by the end of the day. They had cleaned the kitchen, cooked and served dinner, and cleaned again because Mark had forgotten to include "tonight" in the Kitchen Cleaner Signup List. They stumbled back to the Lookout Lodge around 8:30 p.m., expecting to see everyone playing games and being ridiculous, but all they saw when they walked into the living room of Lookout Lodge was a giant brown bear sitting on the couch, eating a slice of pepperoni pizza.

"Don't run," a voice said behind them. Elliot was returning home at the same time, walking slowly up the porch steps.

"Be quiet and still. She will chase you if you run," Elliot whispered.

The door of the Lodge was wide open. That was how the bear had gotten inside. It was so quiet in the Lodge that Mark, Brian and Elliot knew for sure that the rest of the boys had run when the bear walked in, and were probably hiding in their rooms.

"We need to close the door, or it'll get out," Brian said.

"We need to get the bear out," Elliot corrected him. "It can't stay in there."

Mark moaned a little, "But we're out here," he said.

Elliot watched the bear through the window. She was big, real big, but she seemed pretty happy about the pizza. Now would not be a good time to disturb her. He hoped desperately that there were no other bears nearby.

Just then Samantha appeared.

"What are you looking at?" Samantha blurted.

The boys jumped.

The bear jumped, too. It climbed down from the couch and began walking across the room towards the window where the four of them were standing.

The four seventh graders took off. Sam yelled, "This way! I know a good place!" The boys followed her down the wooden boardwalk path and into the secluded church. They closed the door behind them and fell to the floor, breathing heavily, exhausted from shock.

Elliot was the first to stand up. He looked around the room.

"This is a cool place," he said to Sam.

"Yeah, I like it, too," she said. "There's a room in the back you would like. I'll show you later."

"You mean AFTER WE GET RID OF THE
BEAR?" Brian half spoke, half yelled at Sam and Elliot, as
if they had forgotten why the four of them were locked
inside the little church in the first place.

"If only we had a phone or something, we could call
someone inside the lodge, find out what was happening,"
Mark thought out loud.

Just then Samantha had a terrible thought. She looked
at Elliot, her eyes wide open with fear. He knew exactly
what she was thinking. She didn't have to say a word. *Miss
Robles was all alone out there.*

Elliot sat down again. "Aye, Aye, Aye! What is going
on with this place?" He hung his head low and tried to
figure out what they should do. *What would my Dad do?* He
asked himself. *Well that's easy, he'd shoot the bear with a
tranquilizer. But is that the solution?* He wished he could call
his Dad.

The four of them sat in silence, waiting for something
to happen.

A half-hour went by, and the four classmates in the
church racked their brains, brainstorming what they

should do next. Samantha sat before the altar, on the floor with her eyes closed, and prayed. Her mother had taught her that prayer is simply feeling that something has already come true. She started to visualize in her mind how it would feel if they were safe. She felt safety spread across the camp, to all of the seventh graders and Ms. Robles, and suddenly, she started to believe it was true.

"We're safe," she said out loud, her eyes still closed.

"We think," Elliot added, but in a strange way, he felt it, too.

"What's the worst that could happen?" Mark added.

The other three looked at him.

"Let's just go. We'll walk together making a lot of noise, and the bear will run away, and won't bother us at all," Sam suggested.

The three boys were impressed with Samantha's bravery. She was a girl, but she was the first one to suggest that they go out and face the bear.

"And what if it attacks?" Brian asked, very, very seriously.

No one knew what to say to that.

They thought about going outside, but no one was ready to make a move. Suddenly, there was a knock on the door.

"Hey! What are you guys doing?" It was Julian.

"Julian!" Someone opened the door quickly and pulled him inside.

"Whhh…what's going on?" Julian asked them.

"The *bear*. Outside?" Elliot answered.

Julian's face froze. "There's a bear outside?" He asked.

The four of them nodded their heads. Julian dropped to the floor, and lay, frozen solid.

"What are you *doing?*" Mark asked, annoyed.

"Playing dead," Julian answered with his eyes shut.

"*Why?*"

"Because a bear won't eat you if you're dead!" Julian said louder this time, his head raised slightly off the ground, facing Mark, eyes squeezed tightly shut.

Sam and Elliot looked at each other and began to laugh.

"The bear's *outside*, Julian. You're *inside*." Sam laughed.

"Were you in the Lodge?" Brian asked Julian.

"No. V.J. and I just walked back from the kitchen. We were making banana splits. V.J. went inside, and I walked back here because I saw the light on and I had a feeling it was you guys," Julian explained. He opened one eye and stared at the ceiling, as if it was helping him think.

"And you didn't see the bear?" Sam asked.

"No," Julian answered. "Was it *big*?"

"Wait – V.J. walked inside, and he didn't see a bear? Maybe it's gone!" Samantha said.

Elliot just walked in circles, very fast, thinking.

"If the bear is gone, we should go back," he said.

Mark looked him in the eyes and asked, "Are we ready?"

Everyone knew the answer to his question. There was no fear among the kids in the church. They gathered up their things, and stood at the front door.

Samantha had her hand on the door handle, but then stopped suddenly.

"Wait!" She shouted, and ran to the side room in the back of the church where she had hidden the butter knife. She carried it out and handed it to Elliot.

He looked at her strangely and asked, "You want me to kill the bear with a butter knife?"

"No!" Sam yelled at him. "Duh. I just got it for you because I thought you could use it. You know, since you couldn't bring yours?"

Elliot smiled and accepted the gift.

"Thanks."

"We're walking straight to the Lodge," she commanded to her cohorts. "No bears can stand in our way. Make noise, and stay together," she said. Elliot clenched his butter knife, and pushed open the door.

The bear was gone, and the big room was so quiet they could hear the grandfather clock ticking from across the hall.

"Stick together. Let's check out every nook and cranny," decided Elliot. Samantha locked the door behind them, and Julian closed all of the windows tight.

"It wouldn't have gone up the stairs; the stairwell door was closed when we saw the bear."

"Well, we covered the entire downstairs. The bear isn't inside," Elliot said after they carefully and slowly searched for the bear.

They walked down the hallway to let everyone know it was safe to come out.

Afterwards, they took roll, and everyone was there –
even the girls. We had all moved over to Lookout Lodge.
There were plenty of rooms on the second floor, and it
was closer to everything. Holly House was right on the
edge of the forest, and was very dark at night. The
seventh grade assembled in the center room again, feet
sprawled out over couches and chairs, pillows and
blankets thrown at and over each other.

Mark had a few words to say to everyone.

"I'm getting tired of taking care of all of you," he
began. Everyone moaned and grumbled at his words,
because he does this all the time, being a year older, and
much bigger than us all. "No, seriously, just listen. There
are a few rules we all have to follow, before someone gets
killed. First, don't leave food out anywhere. Clean up after
yourself. Just look what being sloppy has done for us so
far. And don't go anywhere alone. We have to stick
together."

Julian spoke, "Isn't it weird that we read an article
about bears, and then saw one?"

Everyone looked at him, puzzled.

"You read an article on bears?" V.J. asked.

"You didn't?" Julian responded.

"No. Mine was about Mount Everest," V.J. answered.

Everyone looked at me and Samantha, and Nicky. We all shook our heads no.

"Mine was about the Louisiana Purchase," Sam said, rolling her eyes.

"I can't remember what mine was about," Nicky said.

I just shook my head no; I still wasn't confident speaking in front of a crowd.

The night wound down after that. Mark's words were well taken. We knew he was right. No one could see any reason to be concerned about what Julian had read. Movies went on, video game tournaments were played, Nerf balls bounced off the walls, ceilings, and people's heads, until the seventh grade eventually dozed off into another night in the wilderness.

7

The next morning, a group of girls went down to the kitchen and made scrambled eggs and buttered toast for breakfast – for everyone. They spread the food out into the warm serving plates behind the cafeteria line, and invited everyone to come over and eat.

It was really nice of them. Most of us went, even Elliot, which is no surprise because he loves to eat.

I sat at a round table with Sam, Julian and Elliot. It was there that I realized Sam and Elliot were keeping a secret. At first, I assumed they liked each other; but that didn't make sense right now. No, their eyes were playing a game, and I was determined to find out what was going on.

"So, are you moving into the church today?" I asked Samantha.

"It's not a church, Nines, it's a sanctuary. But yeah…at some point," she said, then looked at Elliot, and they both laughed out loud.

"What's so funny?" Julian asked.

We both looked at Sam and Elliot fiercely, wanting to know what they were scheming up in their little rebellious minds.

"Nothing," Sam said. Of course nothing was funny. That's why they still could not stop laughing.

"So, you're moving out there all alone? Won't you be scared at night?" I asked Sam.

"No," she answered confidently. "The doors lock. Besides, you guys can move out there, too. Just bring down some beds. We can set them up in that big room. I get the small room in back, though. It'll be fun," she suggested, sounding hopeful that at least one of us would agree.

"Is there a bathroom there?" I asked.

"Yup. And it's nicer than the other ones!" Sam said.

"Julian," Elliot said. "Let's go check it out later this afternoon. If you want to, we can carry some furniture down. I'd rather be there than in that loud mess at the Lodge. It's starting to smell there."

Julian started bouncing up and down in his chair with excitement. "Let's go now! I'm done eating. You ready?"

"I can't go now. I have something to do first. I'll find you when I get back," Elliot said.

Julian asked, "Where are you going?"

And immediately, at the very same time, Samantha and Elliot both shouted, "Nowhere!" and started laughing together again.

We let them go when we were finished eating. Julian and I watched them walk down the dirt road into the woods.

"Should we follow them?" I asked Julian

"Do you want to?" He asked me.

"No. There's poison ivy and ticks and bears in there," I said.

Julian turned away from the forest view and said, "Okay then. I don't want to either. V.J. said there's a soccer game at 10:30 at the field. You can come with me if you want. You don't have to play, just watch."

Everyone knew that I didn't play sports. I had most of my panic attacks in gym class.

"Okay, I'll go. I want to get out of this dining hall before someone asks me to do the dishes!"

We jumped off the wooden stoop, and ran across the grassy yard to the field. Julian joined in the game, and I sat and watched on the sidelines. There was a small group of spectators, and as the sun shone down on us over the tall oak trees, everyone, in that moment, seemed to be happy.

Around 4 o'clock, we heard a rumbling in the distance, and a cold wind carried some grey clouds into camp. Rain. We ran for shelter. Julian and I headed for the dining hall again because we were getting hungry and it was almost dinner time.

When we got inside, Mark and Brian had already set up shop in the kitchen. Brian was carrying the kitchen duty sign-up sheet, trying to figure out who was scheduled to make dinner tonight.

Julian and I sat at a table near the door.

"It's not me," he said. "I'm cooking Thursday."

"I cook tomorrow," I said, breathing heavy from the running.

The rain was pouring down so heavy that we could hear it dropping like pebbles onto the roof. It was relaxing. I felt relieved to be out of the rain. My survival hormones were starting to kick in. The need to be warm and dry left no room for fear or anxiety to creep in on me. But we still had not heard from Sam and Elliot.

"I guess those two are getting wet," Julian spoke up, reading my thoughts.

"They really should have told us where they were going. Should we worry?" I asked him.

"No, because there they are." Sam and Elliot walked into the room, sopping wet and smiling. Elliot came to us and shook his crazy yellow hair out like a dog, spraying cold raindrops on us and our table.

"Stop!" I screeched. It was totally annoying.

"Where'd you guys g…oh wait, I know where you were. Nowhere, right?" Julian asked.

"Exactly," Elliot stated, wrapping his arms around his chest. "Geez, it's cold in here!"

"I'm going back to the lodge to change," Sam said. "Anyone want to come?"

"I have to get something to eat first," I told Sam. "Aren't you guys hungry?"

"No, we ate." Sam said, as she turned and walked out the door.

"Where'd you eat?" Julian asked Elliot.

"I don't know what you're talking about, but I'm going with her," Elliot said, and walked right out the door into the rain.

Julian and I just looked at each other.

"I'll figure out where they were." I promised him. It gave me something to do.

Later that night, the four of us gathered at Sam's place. We found firewood stored indoors near the old stone fireplace, and we lit a fire to keep out the chill that the wind and rain had brought to the camp.

Sam had collected pine cones, acorns and smooth, white stones, and arranged them around the room for decoration. Elliot had shown her some of the plants in the forest that were edible, and she organized the branches and leaves into piles that didn't look much like food to me.

It was still raining, so we couldn't bring our beds down from the lodge, but we set up a campground on the floor with pillows and blankets. Samantha had her own room in the back – a cool one with a bed, desk and bookshelves. But me, Julian and Elliot were happy on the floor near the fireplace.

Sam said to me, "I'm so glad you talk now, Nines."

The others agreed.

"I guess I'm not afraid anymore. I don't know why. It just went away. Isn't it weird that we weren't really friends before, but now we are?" I asked them.

"We weren't allowed to be friends the way that school was run, Nines. That place is a mess." Elliot replied.

"I know!" Sam added. "Now that we are free, I can see so many things I couldn't see before. Look at how well everyone gets along here. Why is that?"

Julian sat up from under his blanket and leaned his elbows on his pillow.

"Because no one is forcing us to do anything we don't want to do. Like read stupid articles and answer stupid questions."

I added, "And do stupid math problems."

And Sam added, "Over and over and over again even if we got them all right."

"And tell us we're wrong, instead of listening to what we say," Elliot said.

We must have thought of a hundred things that were messed up with our school.

"It's not our fault that they think we're stupid," Elliot prophesized. "They just don't understand us. We don't want to live their stupid lives. Here we are, trying to be happy, and we get yelled at."

"I think I've learned more things about life in the past few days then I learned in my entire seven years at Shadyside School," I decided.

"Me too," Sam said.

"Me three," added Julian.

"Me four," said Elliot.

We talked about the little sanctuary, and wondered who it belonged to. We decided that it didn't matter what religion it was made for, anyone could use it for what they needed. Sam said she wanted to have Yoga classes there, and Julian said maybe he could teach a karate class. I liked the church because it was quiet. Green trees surrounded the entrance, and from the inside, all of the big glass windows had a view of the treetops. The books in the back room where Sam slept were interesting – books on plants, cooking, history, and all kinds of interesting new things to learn. I decided that I loved this little place, and I could feel safe here if my friends were here with me.

We were getting sleepy, so we put out the fire and got in our beds. A soft glow of light came through the front window from the outside porch lights. We heard an owl *whoo* outside.

"How long do you think we're going to be here?" Julian asked, talking to the darkness.

"Not much longer," Elliot said, and then someone started to laugh.

"That's it!" Julian shouted, and jumped up from the floor into a superhero karate pose that he had definitely made up himself. "WHAT are you two HIDING from us?"

By now, Sam was laughing so hard from the other room, that we all picked it up like a contagious disease and broke into a four-person giggle fit.

"*Nothing*," Elliot managed to say, through laughing breaths, and that just made all of us laugh even harder.

Eventually, most of the students made their way to the computer lab to take the reading test, so they would be able to email their parents and place an order for more food. Those who had already taken the test and sent mail were still waiting for a reply. It had been a few days, and no response.

One morning, it was raining out, and since we couldn't play outside, a bunch of us went to the computer lab to see what we could figure out. Even Elliot came with us.

"Nines, you said you sent your parents an email, and your inbox is still empty?" Elliot asked me that day.

"They didn't get it," he decided. "No one is getting our mail."

There was a slight buzzing noise in the computer lab as everyone logged in and put on their headphones. We couldn't hear much outside noise, just the voice of our computer teacher Jason, and the music that was played when we got a question right. That's why we didn't know that after Mark finished his reading test, a door opened behind us and Jason told him to go in there and play a video game as his reward.

We were all facing the other wall when he left, so we had no idea.

This is what happened when he got inside, according to Mark.

There was one of those arcade racing games where you sit inside the machine and drive the pedals with your feet and the screen is in front of you, like virtual reality. There was a steering wheel, too, and a huge dashboard all lit up. I sat down and a weird computer voice said, "Close your door and fasten your seatbelt." So I did. "Now, helmet on." And I did that too. Then the car started up and I was playing the game, and then it stopped, and there was Jason, standing in the middle of my racetrack. He actually got out of the blue Porsche. I was the red Ferrari.

He said, "Well, Mark, you've made it this far. Now it's time for a little reading race. Use your strategies and do your best. For each question you get right, you get more time on the track. Good luck. I'll see you at the finish line!" And he got back into his car and drove away. My gas pedal and steering wheel were frozen, so I took the test because I wanted to play again.

I read the first paragraph and answered the question. I guess I got it wrong because it shocked me. The machine shocked me, and the voice said, "You're not reading. Use your strategies and answer the questions." So I kept reading, and it shocked me again. It said "You can't fool a machine, Mark. READ!" and sent this shockwave out of the steering wheel. It went up though my arm and out my foot. I felt like I had been struck by lightning. I tried to take my helmet off and get out of there, but I was locked in. I couldn't get out. That's when I started screaming.

I was banging on the door of the machine, trying to get out, and it kept shocking me. I tried to smash it, break it, but it was indestructible.

"And that's when Elliot found you," I said to Mark.

Elliot told us the rest of the story. "I finished my dumb test and got a D, and figured out that the whole email and food order thing was crap, so I took off my headphones and heard this banging noise in the room next door. There was a sign on the door that said, "Employees Only." I thought, *Good thing I can't read,* and tried to pull open the door. It was locked. I could see Mark in there though the glass and his arms were flying all over the place banging on the arcade game. I tried to find something to smash the glass with, and that's when I yelled to Sam and she started to get everyone else's attention. Julian found the fire extinguisher and I yelled "Get back!" and smashed in the glass. It set off an alarm, but I got my hand through, and unlocked the door. We got inside, and Mark yelled 'Unplug it! It's killing me!' We found the plug and unplugged the monster machine, and got Mark out of there. It was crazy, man."

Mark added, "I couldn't move. I was lying on the ground and I couldn't move my body."

We all bent down around Mark's body and tried to decide what to do.

"What do you do when someone is electrocuted?" Sam asked.

"It's like a burn, on the inside," I said.

Elliot made a decision. "Get on each side of him. We have to carry him to his bed. Nicky, you go get Brian and the rest of the gang and meet us at the Lodge. Nines and Sam, stay here and help us. Be careful. Let's go."

Julian asked, "Can we get electrocuted by carrying him in the rain?"

No one said anything. We thought about it for a minute, and finally Mark yelled up at us from the floor, "No!"

We all found a part of Mark's giant overgrown body to support, and carefully carried him out of the building. At one point I dropped his leg and it was dragging on the ground in the mud. I swiftly got my strength back, though. We carried him across the grassy courtyard, over the sidewalks and bushes, through Lookout Lodge, up the stairs and into room 202. We didn't know if he was okay, or not. He was just sort of lying there helpless, like a giant beached whale.

Everyone pitched in to help. We brought him water and food, searched the camp for medical supplies, found nothing but band-aids, and sat in the living room together, everyone concerned, and a little scared.

"We need the adults," Nicky said. Everyone was thinking it, but no one wanted to say it yet. We had given up trying to contact the adults.

"They tried to kill him," Brian said. "Who's the next one on their list?"

"Anyone who fails the reading test," Elliot revealed. No-one else had thought of that.

"Oh my God," Sam gasped. "He's right! Mark got in trouble for failing the reading test!"

Julian's face went pale. He never set foot in that computer lab again after that day.

V.J. came up with a new idea. "The principal can see us. There has to be some kind of monitor somewhere. We can find it." He walked over to the television screens and started looking behind them, hoping to decipher the code and find the missing link.

Elliot and Sam locked eyes, nodded their heads, and stood up at the same time.

"We'll be right back," Elliot said as they walked away.

There was mass protest.

"Where are you going?"

"You can't leave now!"

"It's raining outside!"

They kept walking. Elliot waved his hand as they closed the door behind them and walked out into the misty forest.

Those of us inside were silent.

"Just let them go," Julian spoke up.

I backed him up with a "Yeah."

Then I said, "Maybe there's a book that can help us. I'm going to the church to look."

I got up to go, and Julian came with me. I thought that was heroic, since just the week before he was afraid of bears, and didn't want to be without his friends.

We had umbrellas and raincoats from the coatroom, and we donned them and walked the slippery wooden boardwalk path to the church. Inside, it was super quiet. We heard raindrops on the roof. Before I looked for books, I had to get my heart glasses, red plastic sunglasses with heart-shaped frames. The lenses were popped out, so I could see indoors. I rifled through my backpack and found them in their special pink case. I wore them for serious reading projects because they made me feel smart.

I found some books on healing, but nothing on what to do if someone is electrocuted. I was afraid for Mark.

While I was reading, Julian practiced his karate poses in the big room. He found his karate belt in his backpack, and tied it around his head like a ninja. I told him it looked good.

"You know something?" I asked Julian.

He turned his head slowly to face me from a karate pose and with one eye open said, "Hmm?"

"I am so mad right now! What kind of parents leave their kids in the wild to die? And what kind of teachers give up on children? School is supposed to be a place where we are nurtured and supported, not abandoned and abused. I…" And then I stopped. I swear, I don't know how I got this, but I finally got it. My glasses started to slide off my nose, but I pushed them back up.

"They don't know, Julian. Our parents don't know! Does anyone have the letter? The envelope they mailed home before the first day of school?"

"Sam does. Her mom gave it to her."

"I'm going through her things, she won't care."

I found the manila envelope that Sam's mother handed to her that night in the kitchen. Inside were all of the papers that the families had received. Some of them were ripped in half, below the dotted line, where the parents had to sign and return, like a permission slip. I read the documents out loud to Julian. We were shocked. The words had been manipulated in a way that made it seem like this really was a school, and that adults were here for us.

"We need to call a town meeting," I said. "We need all minds on deck."

We ran back to Lookout Lodge in the rain, carrying the papers under our raincoats. My left hand held the envelope, while my right hand kept my glasses on my nose as I ran. Julian still had his karate belt tied around his head. He looked like a warrior.

Meanwhile, Sam and Elliot were running as fast as they could to get to Miss Robles for help, jumping over rocks and dodging puddles in the rainy woods. There was no time to talk; they were both lost in thought. Their plan had changed now that Mark had been hurt.

When they arrived at the RV, Sam banged on the door.

"Miss Robles!" Sam screamed. She banged harder. "Miss Robles!"

Miss Robles opened the door and let them in. They stood inside, dripping wet.

"What happened?" Miss Robles asked. She sounded unusually calm.

"Mark got electrocuted by the reading machine. He's going to die if we don't help him."

Miss Robles just looked away, thinking.

"We have to go," Sam insisted. "You have to drive us back. In this."

Miss Robles laughed. "It's too big, Sam! It won't fit down the old trail."

"Yes it will. You could just take the back road," Elliot said sharply. "Or call someone for help."

Sam and Elliot had figured out that there had to be a secret entrance to the camp. Elliot thought it was probably underground.

Miss Robles sat down. She stared out the window. Sam and Elliot were not sure what she was going to do. Finally she spoke.

"You're right. There is more to this than your parents are aware of. Your parents think there are adults here to take care of things. It was Principal McThorn who did this." She looked up at us and said, "I think he made a deal with the government to use you as an experiment. That reading machine is actually a prototype for a new computer that can read minds, which also means it knows when a student is reading, or not reading. McThorn agreed to test it out on your group in exchange for government grant money."

Elliot and Sam felt their rage building up. Adrenaline rushed into their bodies as their anger turned to courage.

Just then, Miss Robles stood up and started looking for her keys.

"Let's go," she said. "Elliot, go outside and close up anything that's loose. Sam, clean up anything inside that can fly around. I think we can squeeze up the trail. It's the only road to the camp."

They got to work. Miss Robles started the engine and the R.V. started to move.

"We'll drive as far as we can," she said, maneuvering the van around boulders and logs. The rain came down harder, and thunder boomed outside. Every now and then Sam and Elliot had to jump outside and move a log or branches out of the road, but eventually they reached the camp with only a few dents in the van. The windshield was covered with wet leaves, with only a tiny space left clear. Sam and Elliot directed Miss Robles to Lookout Lodge. She tore across the lawn and pulled up to the front door, leaving deep skid marks in the grass.

They walked right into the emergency town meeting that we had called.

When the seventh grade saw Miss Robles, we were shocked. Tanya and Nicky both screamed, and then ran up to hug her. Some of the boys were freaked out, so they just sat there. Brian looked at Julian, and then at Elliot, and then at the ceiling. I looked at Julian, and we both finally understood that this is what Sam and Elliot had been hiding from us.

"Mark's up here," Sam said, and led her to his room.

Mark was okay. After the shock wore off, he was just tired. Miss Robles told him he was going to be fine, and somehow, that made him all better. He came downstairs with us, and the meeting continued.

V.J. was still on the floor. He took apart a television, determined to find any sign of communication device, whether ingoing, or outgoing. He was lying on the floor behind the appliances, bending over like a plumber trying to fit under the kitchen sink. He sat up finally, and scratched his head. He looked over at us, then back to the TV, then over at us again, and then this strange look came over his face. He spoke, in a deep, sinister voice. He seemed to be speaking to the stuffed moose head on the wall. He said, "Ladder. I need a ladder." Everyone scattered to try to find a ladder, or anything similar. We came back with chairs, crates and some plastic purple storage containers, but no ladder.

We stacked the chair and a crate beneath the moose head, and V.J. climbed up. He stared deeply into the fake glass eyes, and saw a light.

He climbed down.

"It's in there. Cameras are in the eyes, and microphones in the ears," he said, and sat down, pleased with his work.

The seventh grade crowded beneath the brown furry animal's face.

"Hello?" We yelled at the moose.

"Is anybody listening?"

We waited. The moose said nothing.

At this point, things had changed. The seventh graders wanted answers. The town meeting soon turned into chaos, with everyone trying to monopolize Miss Robles, or throwing footballs at all of the animal heads lining the hallways, seeing if they could knock them down to get inside and look for cameras.

Elliot pulled Sam aside and whispered in her ear, "I'm taking the RV. If you want to come, it's now or never."

Julian and I saw them heading for the door. I said to him, "Don't let them get away."

We followed them outside. No one noticed. Now that Mark was all right, Miss Robles was there, and the cameras had been found, the seventh grade thought they were safe, but we knew something was still not right.

Julian and I caught up with Sam and Elliot just as they were approaching the RV.

"Where are you guys going?" Julian called out to them.

"Grab them!" Elliot yelled to Sam. He picked Julian up over his shoulder and jumped into the RV. Samantha did the same to me, which wasn't hard to do considering her size.

Elliot sat in the driver's seat and said, "Hold on." Sam locked the door and sat in the passenger seat beside him.

"You're abandoning them?" I was shocked. After all this time, I thought Elliot had changed. I thought he wanted to help us, instead of only worrying about himself.

"No talking!" He yelled at me like a mean teacher. "I need to concentrate." He started the engine and got away from Lookout Lodge without making too much noise.

"I turned up the music in there, so they wouldn't hear me start up the RV," he told us, proud of himself as if he was the next 007. "You didn't notice, did you?"

Sam was smiling now. She wasn't worried.

"Don't worry!" She said to me and Julian. "We know what we're doing."

Julian was staring out the window, wondering how Elliot could see through all of the leaves that were plastered to the front windshield after their race through the woods. So this is what they had planned all along.

Samantha began to explain, while Elliot turned back onto the winding dirt paths that led back to Miss Robles' campsite.

"We're rescuing them, not abandoning them," she explained.

"But Miss Robles is here now. Doesn't that mean we're okay? Isn't she going to call home for us?" I asked.

"That's what everyone thinks. That's what we thought," Elliot answered, nodding his head toward Sam. "But there's nothing she can do. This is bigger than her." He said, staring carefully through the mini windshield as he steered around a gnarly branch.

He was an excellent driver.

"She can get into trouble for spying on us," Sam added.

Julian was sitting at the mini **kitchenette**, holding on for his life as we bumped up and down through the forest, trying to put all of the pieces together.

"So, where are we going?" He asked.

"Back to school, of course!" Elliot smiled a huge smile. I had never seen him this happy.

"Can we stop at my house first?" Julian asked, and we all started laughing at our crazy situation.

8

When we reached Miss Robles' campsite, Elliot parked the RV. He left it running, and leaned over to turn on the GPS.

"Now, it looks like she covered the road up with brush. Once this thing tells us where to go, we'll be back on the road." He waited a few minutes, and finally said, "There! Come on!"

We followed Elliot out of the van and ran to a clearing. There was brush, logs and rocks piled up, and underneath it, a road. Julian climbed onto the hood of the van and cleared the leaves from the windshield.

"She's pretty sneaky," I thought about Miss Robles, as I carried a heavy boulder across the road and dumped it into the woods. I wondered why she did this. Was it for us?

We took some of Miss Robles' things and placed them in her tent, including her coffee for the morning. If she decided to come back, she would have everything she needed. But if she needed supplies, she could stay at the seventh grade camp. That way, she would have a clear perspective on what it was like for us, and she could help us when it came time to arrest Mr. McThorn. A pile of books and papers covered the little kitchen table that was built into the wall of the mobile home, so I gathered everything up and shoved it beneath the seats in a cabinet.

The path was clear, and we were moving again.

"I never explored past this point. It was obvious that there was a road somewhere, otherwise this rig wouldn't have been able to get here." Elliot told us. The GPS was directing us off the mountain.

"Wake me up when we get there" Julian requested from the back room. He was sprawled out on the queen-sized bed.

It was a very comfortable mobile home, even the way Elliot was driving.

We drove downhill on a dirt trail for about half an hour, and reached a gravel road. There were no signs of civilization yet, and we continued along the way. Eventually, we came to the highway. Elliot turned onto the ramp, and gunned it.

Elliot was beaming with excitement. His eyes were glued to the road. He looked in both rear view mirrors, and merged into traffic.

"Have you ever driven on the highway before?" I asked him. Anxiety and fear were officially back, lurking in my mind, and I did not feel safe.

"Of course not, Nines!" He said. "I'm only thirteen!"

The ride was much smoother now, and we were able to start planning what to do next. We were two hundred and seventy two miles from Shadyside. Sam and I did the math, and figured it would take about five hours to get back to Shadyside if we drove at fifty-five miles per hour. We would need to get gas eventually. Luckily, Sam had been carrying her money around in her pockets. It was part of their plan to escape.

What to do when we got to Shadyside became the main topic of discussion.

If we went straight to the police, they might not believe us. Not to mention, we did steal an RV and drive it without a license. It would be safer to get an adult first. Sam wanted to get her father, and we all agreed to that. Elliot wanted to make sure that he could be there when they arrested McThorn, but I said it might not happen because the principal is probably prepared to defend himself, after all of those documents he made the parents sign.

Sam and Elliot had not been there when I read the papers to the class at the Lodge. It seems that McThorn had devised a plan to make all of this seem perfectly legal. The permission slips described Jason as our teacher. The words had been manipulated to convince the parents that he would be there with us, without actually stating it. There was a photograph of Jason, and even a biography that described his work experience and training. McThorn also wrote in the agreement that he would be "stopping by often," something he probably wasn't planning to really do.

Everything had a scapegoat. They couldn't prove that the computer had tried to kill Mark, or that our parents had never received our emails. Someone was probably hacking in to everything we wrote, and they would just say it was technical difficulty.

"We need to find Mr. Crane," Elliot said, and it made sense. Mr. Crane had always been a great Assistant Principal. We knew he would never let this happen. He probably had been fooled just like everyone else. "You know, I do my best thinking when I'm driving."

As we were contemplating this mess, we heard Julian crying from the bedroom. Sam and I walked to the back to check up on him, and found him watching a sad movie on Miss Robles' DVD player. It was a tragic love story.

"Don't leave him!" Julian sobbed. We closed the door and left him to cry.

It was starting to get dark when Elliot pulled into a truck stop for gas. It was called The Flying W, and there was a huge parking lot, a restaurant, and a gift shop that had everything you could possibly need on the road. We all got out, stretching and getting some air. We were still far from any towns. We walked through the gift shop and bought some food, filled up the gas tank, and reassembled.

"I'm thinking we should stay here overnight. We can pull into one of the parking areas in the back and sleep," Elliot decided.

"Really?" Julian asked. "We won't get in trouble?"

"No," Elliot answered. "It's a rest stop. That's what they're for. My dad and I have done it a million times. We drove to Alaska one summer when he was working in Denali. There were some nice rest stops on that ride! There's bathrooms here, showers, an arcade, and the diner. There's a pay phone in there, but I don't think we should call home until we come up with a solid plan. Does everyone agree?"

Sam spoke first. "I think it's the best thing to do. We don't want Elliot to fall asleep at the wheel, because then we'd all be dead. I'm okay not calling home yet – we don't want them to freak out. So, I agree."

"Me too," I said.

"Me three," Julian added.

"Me four," Elliot decided, and drove the RV to a corner of the parking lot with a view of the foothills.

That night, I read an amazing book while everyone else was sleeping. I found it in that pile of books I stored in the cabinet under the kitchenette table. I sat in the driver's seat until midnight, under the glow of the green neon "Open" sign blinking in the parking lot, reading *Walden*, by Henry David Thoreau.

The next morning we awoke to the sounds of diesel engines starting up. The rain had stopped, and the truckers were getting ready to go. The sun rose purple and orange over the eastern mountains as we scrambled out to the diner for breakfast. We wore assorted pieces of clothing that we had found in Miss Robles' RV, and carried our wet clothes in plastic bags to wash at the truck stop Laundromat. I thought we must have looked disheveled, until I saw the other people at the rest stop looking worse for wear. As the light grew brighter I noticed several other RVs had parked here for the night as well. I recognized them from the road. They each had their own special name, like a boat. There was *Free Spirit*, *Adventurer*, and *Born Free*. Ours was called *Independence*.

We were having so much fun that we didn't even think about yesterday's problems until we got back to the RV, and had to decide what to do next.

We didn't want to leave. Our newly acquired freedom felt so good. We had passed the point of fear, and learned that we really didn't need to follow anyone else's rules. We never would have learned what we know now if we were still sitting in the cement block classrooms of Shadyside School.

"I miss our people," Julian said, referring to the classmates we left behind. "We were so united at camp. I hope they're okay. Was it mean for us to leave them?"

Sam said, "We're rescuing them. If we hadn't left, we'd still be on that mountain too."

"But what about the moose head with the camera?" Julian asked.

I reassured him. "We don't know if anyone ever heard our messages, Julian. And what is McThorn going to do? Say, 'Oh, sorry kids, my bad, come on back and destroy my school again?'"

"But what if we promise to be good?"

Elliot had a response to that. "There's no way I'm going back to the old ways. I'm done. I'll home school like I did in Alaska. We can do it together. I thought of that when I was driving yesterday. I really get my best ideas when I'm driving!"

We sat at Miss Robles' mobile kitchen table. I took out some paper from her pile and made a chart listing all of the details of our situation, the pros and cons, our resources, strengths and weaknesses. We were quiet for a while letting it all sink in, and then I got it.

I don't know how I got it, but I did.

Home school. United. *Independence.*

Maybe it was the ancient Sumerian Gods coming back to me from Ninevah, or maybe I was inspired by Thoreau. I don't know how, but I got it.

"I got it," I said. I looked up at my travel companions.

"We'll write a Declaration of Independence, for the United Seventh Grade of America." I was smiling so hard that my eyes must have looked like I had just sucked a lemon. "The principal is an absolute despot! We have the proof!"

Elliot loved the idea.

Sam's response was, "How are we going to do that?"

Julian asked, "What's an absolute despot?"

"It was our vocabulary word last year, Julian! Remember? We were supposed to memorize the beginning of the Declaration of Independence."

"I didn't really understand it," Julian replied.

"I didn't know we were supposed to memorize it. I thought we just had to read it," Sam said.

"An absolute despot is someone who rules over people in a cruel way. A tyrant. I'll write the declaration. I understand it because I saw the original one in Washington D.C., when I was there with my parents. You know how they are with history. It's in a glass case, next to the Constitution and the Bill of Rights. The Charters of Freedom, they're called. But I need to go back to the camp and get some books from the sanctuary. With the right research, I can make it better than they ever believed we could accomplish as seventh graders. They think we're dumb, and we have to prove them wrong. Everyone has to sign it, like the original one. We have to go back."

They looked at me, they looked at each other, and they looked at the mobile home. Suddenly, the desire for freedom for the good of the whole was stronger than our need to go home. There was a sudden rush of energy as we all jumped up and got ready to leave. We were going back to the mountain to get our people.

9

Sam and I worked at the kitchen table while Elliot drove and Julian returned to the back room to watch the end of his movie. I write best when I'm alone, so that was fine with me. I asked Sam to skim through some of the books Miss Robles was using for her research project to see if she could find any information to use in our document. I was glad I had my glasses with me, because they help me think.

"Listen to this," Sam said, and read aloud from a book. "Any system that removes the individual from the opportunity for self-growth will have a detrimental effect on that individual and eventually, the world at large."

"That's exactly what our school did to us," I looked up from my papers, adjusting my heart glasses onto my nose. "Sending us away was the best thing they ever did. If only they had included us in the planning, we would've created a much better school. One that was closer to our families, too."

Sam kept reading. "Then it says, 'The current education model imposes ideals onto the child – ideal behaviors, ideal facts and information, which are in most cases, biased toward what the government has allowed to be exposed in schools.' What does that mean?"

"Well for one thing, we don't have freedom of speech in schools. We have it on the street outside school, but not in the actual school building. And there's no freedom of religion in schools. These are basic rights that all Americans have, except children in school." I was getting infuriated. This was good, because it fueled my writing fire. Sam kept digging up some amazing and sometimes scary facts. It turns out that Miss Robles was writing a dissertation for her Ph. D. The title of her paper was "Should Seventh Grade Exist?" In it she argued that there was no "seventh grade," that because of the extreme differences in our growth and development at this age, any attempt to fit us into a standardized mold would fail.

Meanwhile Elliot was up front listening to music (softly, so I could concentrate), and driving along without a care in the world. He had finally found something he loved to do – drive.

"We can go anywhere, now that we're free," he said at one point, not to anyone in particular. It was more like he was dreaming aloud, inspired by the open road, and the sunshine that lit the distant horizon.

We traced our original route back, and arrived at Miss Robles' old campsite. We were prepared for chaos, so we developed a plan of action to avoid any trouble.

First, we hiked back up the wide trail. When we got closer to the buildings, we hid in the woods, and crept around to the back of our little sanctuary. No one was around, so we were able to sneak in without being interrupted.

I found the book that I needed. It was a book about Thomas Jefferson's life, and in the back was a photocopy of the original Declaration of Independence.

I locked myself into Sam's room because I needed silence, and the oak desk with the peaceful view of the forest. We couldn't face our classmates until we had the declaration in our hands, so the other three waited patiently while I drafted the historical document.

I came out at one point carrying the heavy Thomas Jefferson book to say, "We need oak tag."

"Huh?" It was a group response.

"Oak tag!" I yelled. "The heavy ivory-colored art paper we use. There's a stack of it in the art room at Community Hall. Someone has to go!"

Elliot thought that he was the best choice because he was not only sneaky and stealthy, but nobody could mess with him when he had his mind made up. So he walked outside to find the paper.

"Get markers, too!" I shouted out the door as he turned down the wooden walkway.

As I turned back inside, I saw Sam and Julian laughing at me. My red, heart-shaped glasses were crooked on my nose, and one of my barrettes had fallen down so far that it was dangling in front of my face. I had not brushed my hair in two days.

"You laugh now," I said to them sternly. "But some day you'll be reading books about me!" I walked back to my office.

It did not take long for Elliot to find the paper and sneak it back safely. He handed me my tools, then laid out more supplies on the floor.

"We're making a flag!" He said to Sam and Julian. "Here, everybody make one, and then we'll vote which is best.

I was glad they had a project, because I hate to be rushed. My document was done, but the final product had to be flawless. I found a black marker, and hand-wrote the words onto the oak tag paper in my best historical style.

Finally, we were ready to go. We lined up at the door. I held the declaration, and Julian and Elliot held the new flag over their heads. Elliot's design had won. It was a beautiful flag. A huge yellow seven took up most of the space, surrounded by a light green background. Inside the seven was a giant brown bear with a ferocious-looking snarl and a piece of pizza in his sharp claws.

"Our mascot!" Elliot said, pointing to the bear.

We marched over to the dining hall, ready to face the crowds. Slowly they saw us, and chased after us to find out where we had been and what was happening next. We sent messengers to gather everyone together, and set up the chairs in the dining hall into a grand circle.

Everyone helped as we turned the room into a meeting hall. I found a soda and then prepared a table in front.

Once everyone was there and settled, including Miss Robles, we asked them to quiet down, and Elliot spoke.

"Thank you for coming to meet here in this great hall. We are back to bring you a message. It is something important, and it concerns all of you, so please listen. Even if you don't want to listen, just be quiet so that other people can hear. But I'm not the best one to tell you this news, so here's Nines." He looked over at me with a silent, questioning look to see if I was ready to talk. It would be the first time I had spoken in front of a crowd. In fact, most of the group hadn't heard me speak much at all, since I had chosen to be so quiet.

I nodded my head yes, and stepped up to the front of the group to speak. There was a reaction from the crowd, a few gasps, Tanya shouted, "Oh my God, Nines is talking!" and Mark yelled out, "Go Ninety-Nines!!"

"Thank you," I said. I wasn't nervous. I was filled with excitement. "We came back here to tell you guys about what has been happening to us in school. It's something that has gone on for years, but we didn't see it because we were so distracted every day, with all the stuff that went on. I think you will agree with what Sam, Julian, Elliot and I have decided, but you have to decide for yourself, because that is what democracy is all about, freedom of choice, freedom to choose who you are, and what you become."

I continued. "We believe that our choices were taken away from us at Shadyside School. As students, our inalienable human rights were violated. When we are allowed to be who we are, to study what we want to study, say what we want to say and experience life first hand, conflict disappears, because we're happy. Happy people don't fight."

People agreed, and there were a few quiet conversations in the crowd. I gave them a moment to digest what I had said, then continued on.

"So we have written a declaration to present to the principal of Shadyside School," I picked up the large, hand-written paper from my table and held it up for all to see. "It is The Declaration of the United Seventh Grade of America. And that's us."

Elliot held up the flag and shouted "And this is our flag!"

Everybody cheered. It sounded like a football game. There were high-fives, and people got out of their seats. Finally Elliot had to say quiet down, because I was not about to tackle that noise level. They quieted down, and I stood up front, and read them our new truth. This is the original document, in its entirety. It is now on display in a glass case in the media center lobby, which was renamed The Foyer of the Charter of Freedom. Flash photography is not allowed, to prevent fading.

"The Declaration of the United Seventh Grade of America.

We, The United Seventh Grade, have come together through great **adversity** and hardship. The adversity we face is not the freedom we have found in the wilderness, but the beliefs and limitations of schooling itself. We hold these truths to be self-evident, that all students are created equal, no matter what their grades or test scores, that we are born with certain unalienable rights, as listed in the three great American Charters of Freedom, including the freedom to explore our world, whether it be the world outside, or the thoughts and feelings which live inside us.

We believe that since our government derives its 'powers from the consent of the people' as Thomas Jefferson wrote, a school should derive its powers from the consent of the students. Otherwise, this nation will never know the creative potential of future generations. It is our duty to protect future seventh graders from the hardships we endured.

Since the situation we face at school has become destructive, it is our right to **alter** or **abolish** it and begin a new United Seventh Grade, created for the people and by the people, a place where our childhood is not spent in suffering and punishment, but is a time of growth, when we are allowed to explore this world which has been withheld from our view. We want only to know the truth about life. Anything less will only lead to more confusion. If life, liberty and the pursuit of happiness are the inheritance of all Americans, then it's time that we experienced it for ourselves in school, which is the very government institution that shapes the future of society.

Principal McThorn is a despot; he should be replaced with a principal chosen by the students and for the students. The facts of his absolute tyranny include:

He has exiled the seventh grade in an unsafe manner to be killed by bears, each other, and murderous computers. He has lied to parents about the whereabouts of their children.

He has repeatedly forced students to undergo annual state testing that made some students cry, throw up, or worse, stay back a year in school.

He has denied us the privileges known to sixth and eighth graders.

He has deprived us of a true education, which is the right and opportunity to learn who we are, and what our role is in this world.

Therefore, we, The United Seventh Grade of America, assembled here this day, declare ourselves an independent school, free to learn the truth, and absolved from all allegiance to Shadyside School. As a free and independent school, we will create our own community of learners, governed by the adults as signed below. And with this newly gained freedom, we promise to the world, that we will become the best seventh grade that America has ever seen."

I looked up at a silent room of frozen faces. Samantha was crying, and wiping her nose with a beverage napkin. When I looked at her she started laughing, and with that, everyone else jumped out of their chairs and started to cheer. People ran up and grabbed me and started to hug me. Then Mark picked me up and held me in the air like I was the Queen of Sheba. Miss Robles was crying, and everybody was so happy. It was one of those great moments in history that will never be forgotten.

"But wait, you have to sign!" I yelled above the crowd. It took a while to get everyone to settle down and some people yelled, "Shut up!" which didn't exactly flatter our new nation, but got the job done.

With Mark's help, we got everyone to stand in a line, and found enough markers so that each student could sign in their own choice of color, then keep the pen as a souvenir.

As we were doing this, Miss Robles gathered cookies and soda from the kitchen and set them up at a table, so that we could celebrate once the signing was done. Elliot and I went over to her, while Sam and Julian monitored the official signing.

Elliot reached into his pocket and took out the keys to the *Independence*. He held them out to Miss Robles and said, "I'm sorry I stole your RV. We were planning to come back and get you eventually."

She took the keys. "I forgive you, Elliot. In fact, it looks like you are a better driver than I am. I'm the one who put all those dents in it," she said kindly.

"I guess you have to drive us back," he told her.

She looked at him questioningly, with one of her eyebrows up and the other one down.

"Back to Shadyside," I added, in case she had forgotten where we all came from.

A look of comprehension came over her face, and then she started to laugh.

"Oh, I get it. You know what, Elliot? I don't see any reason why you can't drive everyone back yourself. Just keep the speed limit, and you won't get caught."

Elliot and I looked at her like she was insane. I began to think that her time in the woods had made her mental.

"You want to stay here?" I asked, astonished.

She laughed again. "No, Nines. Just tell Mr. Crane where I am. He'll send someone up to get me." Then she whispered, "Besides, you guys are beginning to stink!" She squeezed her hand over her nose. I had to agree with her, but honestly, it was more the boys than the girls.

Miss Robles seemed unusually relaxed. The mountain was a beautiful place, especially now that she had real buildings to use instead of just her tent. She could finish writing her paper up here. It would be perfectly quiet when we were gone. I decided that I would show her the sanctuary room with the beautiful desk that had been so good to me.

"So what happens when I pull into the school parking lot? They'll get me there," Elliot asked seriously. There had to be a way for us to make it work out. The plan had to be seamless, with no room for trouble.

"Ditch the keys and say Jason drove you," she suggested. "After all, he is sort of invisible."

I liked the way she thought! As long as everyone would agree to honor our plan, it was the perfect solution!

"Miss Robles, we need an adult to sign the Declaration to make it official. That way we can be home schooled."

"Your parents will sign, Nines. I'm sure of it. And, I don't think the state will use this one as law." I got her point. Our new school would be a community effort. The events of that day were like planting the first seeds.

Once the signing was done, we hung the Declaration on the wall. People gathered around to read it, and I heard some nice comments, which was a new, motivating feeling. Word spread that we would gather our things up, organize camp throughout the afternoon, and leave for home in the morning.

10

It was a bittersweet feeling to leave our place on the mountain. In some ways, we wanted to stay and play, but security and responsibility were also calling. We met in the dining hall for breakfast, and discussed our plans. When it was time to go, we all said goodbye to Miss Robles, picked up our bags, which were much lighter now that we knew we had to carry them, and went back into the woods to get the RV.

Loading the RV was not as easy as that blue bus. There were twenty of us. Samantha claimed the front seat next to Elliot. Julian claimed the back bedroom, but chose five other friends to fit in there with him for the duration of the ride. Everyone else found a place to sit. Four squeezed around the kitchen table, and the rest just found a place on the floor. I went in last, so as not to be claustrophobic. I wanted to be near the exit door in case of emergency, so I sat up front near the passenger seat.

Elliot was in his glory, bouncing down the trails, revving the engine when we hit pavement, and finding good songs on the radio. The boys in the back were playing DVD's really loud, and joking around. It was a fun ride. I found room fragrance spray in the bathroom to cover the odors, and opened the windows for oxygen.

We stopped at the Flying W for gas and food, but told everyone to be subtle and not draw attention to our situation. We couldn't use the pay phone to call home. If the wrong parent found out what we were doing, it could ruin the whole plan, so Mark stood by the pay phone at the gas station to make sure no one broke the promise.

Finally, we were on the road again. Our estimated time of arrival at Shadyside School was approximately 2:15 p.m. The students would be in period seven. Perfect number, I thought.

When we pulled off the highway and into our town, everything looked different to me. I was seeing things from a new perspective, I guess. Now this town felt more *mine*. The stores and restaurants and parks that passed by the window were places I was free to explore, instead of being someone else's baggage, or waiting for someone else to decide what to do.

Excitement was building as we rounded the bend towards school. Sam stood up from the front and yelled,

"Everybody get ready! And remember the plan! We're almost there!"

People scrambled to get their things. We had to hide the RV. We knew it would be obvious that we stole it, but we also knew that anyone who knew the truth about our abandonment would not be pressing us for details. Miss Robles had the second set of keys, and she said she'd be back to get the RV in a day or two.

Elliot parked the RV in the far parking lot, in a spot hidden from view of the building. We stood together and walked towards the school, our flag flying high above our heads, attached to an old broom stick with duct tape. Brian was the flag bearer, and each of us wore a badge on our sleeve, smaller replicas of our gorgeous flag that a group of kids had made the night before.

Brian loved the flag and said to the group as we walked, "We are the bears. We are ferocious and strong. Bears!"

We walked straight into the office and past the principal's secretary. Heads turned, grownups gasped, people grabbed for walkie-talkies. The principal was not there, but we knew he was on his way now that the message was sent through the school's security channels. But we didn't speak yet; it was part of the plan.

We moved outside to the courtyard, followed by the entire office staff and the head custodian Mr. Walters. V.J. took the opportunity to sneak out of line, and while the rest of the adults were distracted, he turned on the school-wide loudspeaker and announced, "Attention students and teachers, this is V.J. The seventh grade has returned. Please report to the courtyard for a very special presentation." Then, he locked himself in a vacant office, and began to call all of our parents from the list of phone numbers we gave him during the drive back.

At this point, the principal was yelling at a security guard from a corner of the courtyard. They marched over towards us, and Principal McThorn began to yell at us through a bullhorn.

"All seventh graders, report to the office. All seventh graders, report to the office now."

We ignored him of course. I decided at that point, that he was a crazy person, and whoever couldn't see that, must be crazy, too.

The Assistant Principal, Mr. Crane, appeared, letting the students and teachers pass by him as they walked towards the crowd. His main concern had always been safety, and since there was no harm in us appearing, he did what he should do, which was simple crowd control. Elliot found him and went over to him for support.

"What a surprise, Elliot. What's all this about?" He asked.

"He was trying to kill us, and we escaped. I guess we're smarter than everyone thought," was Elliot's answer.

Elliot told Mr. Crane everything – except the part about stealing the RV and driving it six hundred and twenty four illegal miles.

When he realized what was happening, Mr. Crane extracted the bullhorn from the hands of the crazy principal, and stood on the podium with us. The seventh graders stood on the top of a grassy platform, while the rest of the crowd gathered around.

"Quiet down, everyone, so we can get started." The noise was mostly children talking loudly, and calling out to their friends and siblings across the crowd. The teachers were talking, too, but constantly monitoring for safety, which is one thing that most teachers are very good at.

"Quiet please," he said, until everyone was listening.

"The seventh graders are back, and they have a special presentation for you. So please give them your respect and attention."

He handed the bullhorn to Elliot, who handed it to me, and I handed it to the person next to me like a hot potato. I didn't want to talk to that crowd! Finally Mark grabbed it and stood at the front. We passed him the official Declaration. He was going to read. The lowest scoring reader in the seventh grade was the one who would read it to the world for the very first time. (He had practiced it for the whole ride home.)

"Thank you, Mr. Crane. Teachers, students and staff, we are gathered here today to celebrate a new beginning. Our visit to Shadyside will be short, because we have work to do outside school, at our houses, and in the community. You see, the new school that we were sent to was a huge success, and we finished our work faster than expected. We're on to the next enrichment experience, which I will read to you now. Nines, can you come here for a minute?"

I was mortified, but I walked up and stood next to Mark in front of the whole school. He put his big heavy hand on my back which felt very supportive, and I was grateful for that.

He said, "This is Nines. She is a great writer, like Thomas Jefferson, who wrote The Declaration of Independence. When you see her again, know that you are in the company of greatness."

Wow, I thought. That was so unnecessary, but so very cool. Everybody clapped for me, and I realized that a tiny, simple thing like the words you say about a person can change someone's life forever.

Then Mark read the declaration, and everybody listened. There was a sense of awe and amazement throughout the crowd. The younger kids didn't necessarily understand it, but the teachers, and older kids did. When he was finished, everybody clapped for us and the teachers started corralling students back to the classroom to finish whatever lesson it was that we had interrupted.

Our parents soon began arriving, and as the crowd began to thin, I saw a man in a black suit running towards the parking lot. It was McThorn, taking off before the press arrived.

The rest of the day is just a blur. I remember saying goodbye to everyone as they went off in their parent's cars, feeling sad. It felt like the last day of school, when you were so happy for summer vacation, yet sad to say goodbye to the good things you'd leave behind.

Some parents took the initiative and were swarming the office, demanding to know the truth. But no one there knew anything, or at least they didn't admit to it. In that way, it was good to be a kid again. Whatever mess that lay ahead of the school now was not our problem. We were free, to live and learn in the school called life.

Glossary

(These are my own definitions, as they are used in the story.)

abolish - to get rid of something for good

adversity - something that's hard to deal with; hardship

alter - to change

cuneiform - an ancient form of writing, done with sticks on clay tablets with lots of lines and dots

exodus - a journey that causes a transformation; an escape

gi - Japanese word for karate uniform

Holocaust - the time in history when Hitler killed millions of innocent people

kitchenette - tiny kitchen, in our case one that fits into an RV

omniscient - when the narrator of a story knows everything, including the thoughts and feelings of all the characters

therapist – a person who helps people with their problems

Book Study Questions

1. In the beginning of the story, we learn that Nines chose to be silent in school for two years, because she felt that her words were not respected by her peers, and even some teachers. This is one of her **character traits.** Have you ever felt this way? What are some other **character traits** that you recognize in Nines? How do they change at the end of the story, after her experience on the mountain?

2. Imagine that you are a seventh grader, and you just heard that you will be going away to a new school. You are only allowed to bring one small suitcase, and no electronic equipment. What would you bring? Make a list of everything you would pack in your suitcase.

3. Nines decided to write a glossary, because she wanted to make sure her readers were able to understand all parts of the story. What did you think about the glossary? Did you see any other words in the story that you think she should add?

4. Now that the seventh graders are home, they plan to start their own community school. What are some of the things that you would choose to learn about if you created your own school? How would you design your own school? Research the home schooling resources in your own town for new ideas.

Gratitude

I am deeply grateful to the people who have supported me during the process of creating this book. I love my family and friends, and I appreciate every little word or deed that led to this final product. I am especially grateful for my sister Christine. You are amazing! And my sister Amy, who was the first one to ask me if she could read my draft-in-progress. That was years ago, and the story looks much different today than it did then! To Allison Coulson, for our bookstore meetings and your expert advice, thank you. Christine Caruso, thank you for the proofreading and blessings.

~ *Alyssa*

Alyssa Raffaele earned her Bachelor of Fine Arts in Creative Writing, and Master of Science in Education. She is an award-winning teacher, and lives near the warm, sunny beaches of southwestern Florida. You can contact Alyssa, find more of her books, and read her latest blog posts at **www.alyssaraffaele.com**.